"I'm so glad you've returned, Jess, because you're the only other person on God's green earth who knows what I've been through," Mamie said.

I grabbed for her across the table, spilling my glass of milk and both of our beers and upending my pot pie. As everything splattered onto the floor, I wheeled her around and pinned her against the wall, scattering the copper-bottomed pots with jarring clangs.

I intended merely to hold her there and look into her eyes while I asked her to tell me what had happened to her, but she whispered my name and kissed me.

I had made love to plenty of women in my time, but I didn't know whether the same was true for Mamie Todd.

She sensed my hesitation, so she kissed me again, her lips open and inviting, and I wasn't so stupefied that I couldn't take advantage of it, whether she meant me to or not.

I pulled her to the floor and we embraced, banging against the pots and slipping on the milk and beer. We discarded clothes with passionate haste, and as her smooth skin ran like silk against mine, I knew what resurrection was.

She was lips and teeth and tongue, she was fingers and nipples and thighs, she was satisfaction and temptation and plunder.

PAYBACK

by
CELIA COHEN

THE NAIAD PRESS, INC.
1995

Printed in the United States of America on acid-free paper
First Edition

Editor: Christine Cassidy
Cover designer: Bonnie Liss (Phoenix Graphics)
Typesetter: Sandi Stancil

Library of Congress Cataloging-in-Publication Data

Cohen, Celia, 1953 -
Payback / Celia Cohen.
p. cm.
ISBN 1-56280-084-1 (pbk.)
1. Lesbians—Southern States—Fiction. I. Title.
PS3553.O4188P39 1995
813'.54—dc20 95-14527
CIP

About the Author

Celia Cohen is a newspaper writer who lives in Delaware. She is the author of the best-selling *Smokey O*.

CHAPTER ONE

Dusk was coming as the bus, exhaling dust and fumes, stopped in a little tourist-trap town along the banks of the Lazy River.

I had a ticket for the crossing, which would take me over a natural stone archway to Mason County and the memories that slumbered restlessly there. I had the ticket, but I didn't have the nerve.

The bus driver eyed me curiously as I trudged up the aisle to alight. He had sold me the ticket himself to Mason City, the county seat, still some ten miles away over a two-lane road so weather-worn and neglected that a “Keep Out” sign couldn’t have done more to discourage visitors. It was the way Mason County liked it.

“Evening, ma’am. Getting off here?” he asked.

“Yes.”

“That ticket’s for a weekend fare. Cost you more to ride tomorrow.”

“How much more?” I asked.

He squinted, mentally calculating.

I reconsidered. It didn’t matter what he said. Whatever the amount, I didn’t have it. It wouldn’t be the first time I had nothing but feet for transportation. “Never mind. I’m getting off.”

“No place to stay here,” he said.

I shrugged. It wouldn’t be the first time for that, either.

“Suit yourself,” he said.

I stepped off. The bus lurched and backfired and rattled away, submerging into the twilight that still screened me from Mason County. A chorus of cicadas sang its unrelenting summer song.

I was left in the little town of Stone Bridge, named for the natural archway over the Lazy River. Its main drag was an uneven slab of shops — a hardware store, a drugstore, a newsstand and a couple of woebegone souvenir places selling little copper models of the bridge. Tourists used to pause here regularly, to see the rough span hanging over the curling muddy waters, but when the interstate opened, it stole all but the hardiest away.

I knew this town from childhood, when family outings on Sunday often meant a drive from Mason City to the Stone Bridge Drugstore & Fountain for root beer floats, reputed to be the largest in the state.

My mother, father and I waited patiently for our treats amid the tourists there. We smiled and nudged one another when the unfamiliar clipped syllables of the Yankees cut through the Midwesterners' flat vowels, as level as the Great Plains they lived on, or trampled over our own cotton-soft speech. Sometimes, rarely, a Canadian would thrill us by speaking French.

The town stubbornly had refused to change, hunkering down and waiting for the tourists to return. Brooklyn had a better chance of getting the Dodgers back, but Stone Bridge was prepared to spend the time.

I noticed one place that hadn't been there before — a cafe with a defiant red-and-white checked awning amid the dilapidation. Its name, in white curlicue letters on its broad window, was Mame's.

I had figured on going to the drugstore for a cup of coffee, but the name on the little cafe reminded me of someone I once knew. It was enough to draw me in.

The lone waitress glanced at a clock when I entered, and I knew I had trespassed into the narrow bank of minutes near closing time, when she would rather go home than wait around for another paltry tip. She was filling salt shakers, and all the little tables were already set for breakfast, their delicate chairs with hearts carved on the backs neatly pushed in.

I selected a stool at the counter. "Can I get a cup of coffee?" I asked.

The waitress brushed hair from her forehead with the back of her hand. "It's pretty hot out there. Wouldn't you rather have a Coke?"

"Thanks, but I'd prefer coffee."

"I don't have any made. You'll have to wait for a fresh pot."

"I'll wait."

Irritated, the waitress slapped a salt shaker on the counter. When she banged the metal coffee holder down, a woman's voice called from the back, "Is anything the matter, Honey?"

I stiffened. I knew that voice. Through the years people can go gray or wrinkled or soft as dough, but the voice stays, immutable as a fingerprint.

That voice belonged to Mamie Todd, the very same woman I had imagined when I saw the name of the restaurant and never expected to see again. Nor was I ready to see her again.

She came through the kitchen door before I could bolt. She gasped when she saw me. A stink bomb in church couldn't have caused us as much consternation.

Mamie recovered first. It was, after all, her restaurant, and she was supposed to be there. I was the one the fates dragged in.

"Cross my heart and hope to die, if it isn't Jess Marceau!" she said, her hand placed bewitchingly on her breast.

"Mamie. Mamie Todd," I answered. I nearly smiled, but it was beyond me.

Instead, I remembered why I was coming back to Mason County. I remembered the courtroom, almost five years ago, when the bailiffs led me away in full view of a titillated, if not scandalized, crowd. I remembered that Mamie Todd had been part of that crowd.

"I was just going," I said. "Don't bother with the coffee."

"Jess, wait," Mamie said, then spoke to the waitress. "Why don't you go, Honey? I'll close up."

"Thank you, Miss Todd," the waitress said. "I'll see you in the morning."

When the door had shut and we were alone, Mamie said, "You can have all the coffee you want, Jess."

The kindness in her voice gave me courage, and we studied each other without regard for polite convention. She saw someone sad-eyed and wan, clad in faded jeans and a frayed shirt, open at the neck, and holding a small duffel bag containing everything I owned. I saw someone with short dark hair and dark eyes, as attractive as an artist in love would draw them. Mamie was wearing shorts and a blouse with a pattern of tiny flowers in it that fell off her shoulders. She was as pretty as I remembered her, except there seemed to be a shadow in her almost as dark as the one that haunted me.

"Jess, when was the last time you ate?"

My urge to flee had passed, and I pondered. I couldn't recall a meal since I boarded the bus. "I can't say exactly. I eat when I remember to, or when I have the money. I stay alive."

"I had chicken pot pies for the special today. Come in the back and I'll heat one up for you."

She put the "closed" sign in the window, and I followed her into the kitchen, watching her hips pumping against her shorts. Back in high school, Mamie had been the catcher on the softball team that went to the state championships, almost twenty years ago. As she walked, you could still see the athlete in her.

The thoughts I was having were enough to get me arrested for a felony in some states, including this one.

The kitchen was as spotless as a scientific laboratory. A spit-and-polish chrome work station occupied the center of the room, and the wall near the grill and stove was hung with all manner of gleaming copper-bottomed pots. I sat at a wood block table where Mamie was making a list of supplies she needed. She put a pot pie into a microwave.

"You know," I said, "I came in here because I thought of you when I saw the name of the place. But I never expected to find you running a restaurant. When I left town" — *in handcuffs,* I could have added — "you were a hotshot lawyer."

"Times change," she said briefly and let a silence in.

I tried another topic, teasing her the way I did when we were growing up in Mason City. "I never would have figured you for the conservative type, but you kept calling that waitress 'honey.' "

"Because it's her *name,* you dummy. Honey. Honey Chiles. Can you imagine saddling someone with a name like that?" She laughed. "Hey, I've got some beer in the refrigerator. Owner's private stock. You want one?"

"I don't drink."

"Sorry. Had to quit?"

"No, I just stopped. I stopped everything. I

stopped drinking, I stopped reading, I stopped going to movies, I stopped listening to music, I stopped watching television, I stopped following the news. I don't even bother with the weather reports."

I had meant to sound defiant. Instead, I was drawn to the sympathy in her eyes and ended softly, almost apologetically.

"What do you do?" she asked gently.

"I drift. I take menial jobs where the boss doesn't ask too many questions about me. I work in restaurant kitchens, clean offices at night, wipe down cars at car washes. I'm a good worker, always getting in on time, polite, industrious. I work until the boss wants to promote me or someone starts getting curious about me, and then I move on."

The microwave beeped. Mamie served me the pot pie with a glass of milk. "What do you do for entertainment?"

"I take long walks. If I'm in a town with a minor league baseball team, I go to the games. The players seem so eager, the way people are before life gets a hold of them." That last was more than I meant to say. Something was happening here, and I decided to let it. "Maybe I will have a beer," I said.

Mamie fetched two long-neck bottles from a refrigerator and set them on the table with two glasses. After so much time, one deep swallow made my head fuzzy, although it may have been more imagined than real. It was hard to tell, since I'd allowed myself so little these last five years.

"Taste good?" Mamie asked.

"You bet. You'll corrupt me."

"One person's corruption is another's salvation."

"That sounds like lawyer's talk."

Mamie grimaced. "I'm not a lawyer, Jess. I'm disbarred."

"You can't possibly have said what I think you did."

"I did say it. I'm disbarred, Jess. I'm disbarred for the same reason you went to jail."

Now it was my turn to grimace. All my resolve to suffer in silence was shattered. "I didn't do it, Mamie. I swear to God, I didn't do it!"

"I know, Jess. That's what I mean. You were set up, the same as I was."

It wasn't the beer that made me feel evil spirits rising about me, and it wasn't the night vapors, either. It was being so close to Mason County and the dread that still festered there.

"You were set up?" I asked.

"Yes."

"By . . . did she . . . was Sen —" I could not bring myself to say the name.

I had a clear picture in my mind, though, of Senator Darlene Christmas, the fourth generation of her family to serve in the state legislature, the beauty queen who was crowned at the senior prom and Homecoming and every May Day, the brain who gave the valedictory at commencement and captained the debate team, the head cheerleader and the pride of the Sunday school who memorized more Bible verses than anybody, including Mamie. Our classmate.

Darlene Christmas was the embodiment of Mason County's richest and most powerful family. They controlled the county board of commissioners and the courts, served as trustees for the schools, the church, the hospital and the library, owned most of the real estate, passed out the liquor licenses and gave generously to the local charities. They had done so ever since they drove out the Mason family in the upheaval following the War Between the States, which in these parts still was known as the War of Northern Aggression.

Darlene Christmas. She had a smile as fair as an angel or as mortal as a nuclear winter. I had seen both.

Darlene Christmas had done me in.

"I'm so glad you've returned, Jess, because you're the only other person on God's green earth who knows what I've been through," Mamie said.

I grabbed for her across the table, spilling my glass of milk and both of our beers and upending my pot pie. As everything splattered onto the floor, I wheeled her around and pinned her against the wall, scattering the copper-bottomed pots with jarring clangs.

I intended merely to hold her there and look into her eyes while I asked her to tell me what had happened to her, but she whispered my name and kissed me.

I had made love to plenty of women in my time, but I didn't know whether the same was true for Mamie Todd.

She sensed my hesitation, so she kissed me again, her lips open and inviting, and I wasn't so stupefied that I couldn't take advantage of it, whether she meant me to or not.

I pulled her to the floor and we embraced, banging against the pots and slipping on the milk and beer. We discarded clothes with passionate haste, and as her smooth skin ran like silk against mine, I knew what resurrection was.

She was lips and teeth and tongue, she was fingers and nipples and thighs, she was satisfaction and temptation and plunder.

I knew I must have seemed skinny and pale to her, my buttocks and breasts hardly worth bothering with, while she had a roundness I could drown in. She clasped her hands behind my head and drew my mouth to hers, her tongue seeking mine, and I forgot about how I must have looked as my body came alive.

Clumsy in our ardor and unashamed of desire, we were like lovers who had given each other up for dead.

My mouth roamed over her. She laced her fingers through my hair to guide me. I lingered at her breasts. I kissed her so long my lungs burned, and we gasped for air and laughed.

She was everything I ever dreamed about, a fantasy brought to life with a woman I had yearned for. Those five lonely years I spent wandering in the wilderness suddenly had meaning and purpose.

She cried out when I stroked her and barely hesitated afterwards, for she was as eager as I was. I was impatient and directed her hand and exploded in quick release.

I wanted her again, but she shifted away. "One more move, and I'm going to roll onto the pot pie," she said.

We laughed as hard as we had made love.

I propped myself up so I could look at her. I could hardly believe what had happened. "This is a fine time to ask," I said, "but did you ever get married?"

"No. Never. You?"

"I'm not the type."

"I know. I was just checking."

"Mamie, have you ever been with a woman before?"

"A few times. Opportunities are scarce."

I touched her breasts tenderly, marveling that she had wanted to be with me. "I never thought you would, with me," I said.

"You dummy. I've had my eye on you since we were in the eleventh grade. I used to go to the tennis matches to watch you."

"You did? I thought you showed up to see Collin." Collin was the captain of the boys' team.

Mamie shook her head. "No, it was you."

"But you were always going out with some hunk or another. You always had a date for dances and the football games. I was never in the picture."

"My mother kept making me go out with the boys from Sunday school, and I went because I was afraid of going to hell then. You were always in the picture, from my perspective. I just didn't have the courage."

"Did you ever go to bed with any of those boys?"

"I hardly let them do anything. I was afraid of going to hell for that, too."

"I expect you'll go to hell now."

"I expect I've been there, and so have you. How many people can say they were brought together by jail and disbarment?"

"That's not funny."

"I'm sorry. Jess, why did you come back? You

weren't ever supposed to come back. Senator will crush you like an eggshell as soon as you cross the county line."

"I know, but I had to. I couldn't keep running anymore, even if she ruins me all over again."

"I wish we could get back at her."

"It's impossible."

"Maybe not. Maybe we'll come up with something."

A payback? It was worth thinking about.

CHAPTER TWO

We had much to sort out, Mamie and I, not the least of which was her kitchen.

"Here," she said, handing me a mop, pail and broom, "you said you worked in restaurants. Let's see how you do."

She sat in a chair to complete the list of supplies she needed. I swept away the broken glass and pot pie crusts and then mopped up. I washed the pans we had knocked over and put them back on their hooks. I scarcely paid attention to what I was doing. In my mind I was still on the floor with Mamie.

She interrupted my reverie to say, "You can stay at my place tonight, if you'd like."

"I'd like that very much. Thank you."

"Where were you going to stay?"

"I hadn't thought that far."

"You hadn't thought that far?"

"No, I hadn't thought beyond having a cup of coffee."

"Jess, what's happened to you? You used to have one of the finest minds in Mason City."

I shrugged.

"Do you know who the governor is?"

"Why should I? Ex-cons can't vote."

"I can see you are going to be a serious reclamation project."

"What makes you think I'm capable of being reclaimed?"

"Because you came in here when you saw my name, that's why."

I smiled, and it felt so strange I was conscious of it. Years had gone by since I'd had such a giddy reaction. "I always did like you, Mamie."

The night had closed in on Stone Bridge as we left the restaurant, seeing our way by the soft glow of the security lamps in the stores. Those lights were nothing but an affectation. Not one of those shops had anything worth stealing.

The night air was a busy place. The Lazy River lapped rudely at its banks, like an urchin with bad table manners, while the fireflies lolled and flickered amid the whine of the mosquitoes. Fat ghostly moths, as soft as feathers, dove and fluttered in brainless distraction. Somewhere out there, an insistent chorus tattled that katy-did-it.

"There's nothing silent about the South at night, is there?" Mamie said, as a hard-shelled insect crunched under her shoe.

" 'There midnight's all a-glimmer,' " I said impulsively, quoting Yeats.

She caught the literary allusion and smiled. "Maybe you're not so brain-dead after all," she said and gave me a sidelong look, quite fetching.

Mamie owned a little white Ford. As I tossed my duffel bag into the bag seat, I remembered she had driven a big black boat of a Buick when she was a deputy prosecutor in the county attorney's office. Well, she didn't wear shorts that rode up her thighs then, either. I looked at her legs on the seat beside me and decided that maybe the trade was worth it. And I was sitting a hell of a lot closer to her than I could have in any damn Buick.

Mamie had a place about five miles out of town. Her house, modest but new, sat on a spacious wooded lot that gave her privacy and shade.

"When I was disbarred, I took all the money I had and built here," Mamie said. "I told myself, they may have run me out of Mason County, but they're not running me any farther than this."

I nodded in admiration. She'd made out better than I had, drifting for five years. Then again, she hadn't gone to jail.

She admitted us to the kitchen, and after she flipped on the light, I was startled to see the sturdy wooden table and benches that her family had owned when we were growing up. I shivered as though someone had put a hex on me. Everything that reminded me of Mason City seemed to be having that effect. I was a fool to come back.

I thought we would talk. I wanted to find out why she was disbarred, and I wanted to tell her what Senator had done to me. I wanted to be friends again. I hadn't had one for a long time.

Then she asked me, "Do you want anything?"

"Yes," I said, more with my eyes than my voice. The talk could wait.

Mamie smiled. She took my hand and led me to her bedroom, occupied in a most inviting manner by a canopied, four-poster bed with a row of soft pillows and proper white sheets just begging to be mussed.

"I'm not sure I'm as interested without the pans and pot pies," I said.

Mamie turned down the bed. Tenderly she unbuttoned my shirt, unzipped my jeans and helped me out of my clothes. As I slipped onto the sheets, she shed her shorts and top, her bra and panties, and then lay beside me.

Our lovemaking was slower this time, more genteel really, more in keeping with the dreamy pace of the starry night, with the heat and the whispery moths beating against the window screen. Raising myself above her, I kissed her and moved my mouth in a slow rhythm along her body, while she moaned softly and stroked my skin with gentle fingers.

I was fevered with the scent of her, headier than the dearest perfume.

"Yes," she said, and "yes," and "Jess, yes, Jess, yes, please, yes," as though I needed urging to do what I was being driven to do.

I cared more for the time than I had back at the restaurant. I wanted to tarry in this swirl of passion more than I wanted the explosion of climax. I had been alone for so long that I wanted to memorize the sensations, so I'd never forget what it was to make love to her.

Mamie seemed to understand. She kept me aroused long past what my stamina should have been, until I lay limp and sweating against the sheets.

I slept in tranquillity, something I hadn't done since the day Senator summoned me to her office and said, "Jess, these gentlemen are with the State Bureau of Investigation. They have some questions to ask you."

Mamie was gone the next morning when I reluctantly allowed the sun to coax me awake with affectionate insistence. By custom I was an early riser, a light sleeper, but there was nothing customary about what had happened to me since I'd seen Mamie's name in white curlicue letters on the cafe window and sought solace in a cup of coffee.

She had left a note for me:

Dear Jess,

Sorry I had to leave. I've left you breakfast in the kitchen, and don't worry, I remember how much you used to hate eggs!

I don't serve supper on Mondays, so I should be home by two-thirty, and we can have a late lunch together.

Love you,
Mamie

P.S. Why don't you just relax until I get back? M.

I understood the postscript. Mamie was concerned

I would collect my duffel bag and wander off. Well, I was done wandering. I had come back for better or for worse. This was Jess's last stand.

I wasn't particularly hungry. Even in my better days, food was never much of an attraction. It turned out to be a powerful advantage in those six months I spent in prison, where every meal was a reminder that you were vermin and they expected you to eat like one.

I made myself a cup of coffee, ladled in the cream and sugar, and settled myself on Mamie's screened-in back porch. It overlooked a short stretch of lawn that faded into a scrubby woods of forlorn pines and stunted hardwoods, festooned with drapings of Spanish moss. It looked as forsaken as a room hung in sheets and cobwebs.

There were squirrels and bright birds and an occasional rabbit. I watched them when I had a mind to, and they darted and scampered in a purposeful way, as though there was some plan to God's universe and they had their lowly part to play. Otherwise, I reflected on the circumstances that had brought me here, just a shiver away from Senator Christmas.

There was no one in Mason County waiting for me. My mother and father, Ruth and Hector Marceau, had simply withdrawn and died — of grief, I was certain — not long after my conviction. I told them I was innocent, but I'm not sure they really believed me. They were too overawed by the Christmas family to conceive of it.

They had settled in Mason City to seek work, moving away from the main branch of the Marceau family in New Orleans before I was born. My father was an accountant at the Mason County Commercial Trust, the bank established by the Christmases. My mother worked at the public library, which received a sizable contribution every year from whoever the current Senator Christmas was. The check was presented in a charming ceremony, photographed and reported by the Mason County *Crier*.

I was their only child. We lived in modest but well-bred style, mindful that the Marceaus had their place in the Southern aristocracy before the Yankees despoiled an entire culture.

My very name was a reminder of that past. "Jess" was a family surname, turned into a Christian name some generations back and bestowed without prejudice on Marceau boys and girls alike. I had a grandmother named Jess and an uncle named Jess and assorted cousins, of various ordinals and times removed, named Jess. A lover once suggested the confusion surrounding my name accounted for my sexual disorientation.

I heard Mamie's car turn onto the gravel driveway. She entered through the kitchen, set something on the table and then walked with quickening steps through her house until she spied the open porch door. I caught the expression of relief on her face when she found me, out of fear that I had bolted.

"You didn't eat," she said.

"I had some coffee."

"Is that what you live on?"

"I've been known to."

"What have you been doing?"

"Thinking about how lucky I am to have found you."

"No, you haven't." She looked at me for a long time, taking in whatever there was to see. Not much, I imagine. Eventually she said, "Come inside, Jess, I've got something for you."

She had bought me white slacks, a belt and three shirts in pastel shades of yellow, blue and green.

"You didn't have to do that," I said.

"Oh yes, I did. Have you had a good look at yourself lately?"

I shucked off my clothes, kicked them into a corner and put on the new ones, selecting the green shirt. I liked the way she watched me.

"Once we get you a haircut, you'll look practically human," Mamie said approvingly.

She brought to the table plates of cold chicken and ham, biscuits and a bean salad. She poured a pitcher of milk. Roused by her company, I ate.

"Let's talk," she said.

The glasses of milk gave way to bottles of beer, and the bottles of beer to cups of coffee. We had a great deal to say, Mamie and I.

CHAPTER THREE

When I was a child, I thought December 25 was a holiday to honor the Christmas family. It seemed only natural that the patrons who put flowers on the graves of the Confederate dead, organized the Maypole and sponsored the fireworks on the Fourth of July should have a day of their own and the power to summon Santa Claus.

I don't remember how I got it straightened out, but I wasn't very old when I learned Santa Claus was myth, Baby Jesus was faith, and the Christmas family was enduring.

I was about ten the first time I recall a Christmas patriarch dying. It was Darlene's grandfather, Robert Lucas Christmas, a former senator and justice of the state Supreme Court. Our teacher told Darlene how sorry she was in front of the whole class and had us all tell Darlene how sorry we were, too. Darlene was brave and didn't cry. She was already on her way toward becoming a public figure.

The flag flew at half-staff, and the bank was closed the day of the funeral. The governor came, leading a procession of dignitaries that included the lieutenant governor, the attorney general, members of the Cabinet and dozens of legislators, judges and lawyers. The Mason County *Crier* ran extensive coverage with text and photographs framed on black-bordered pages.

For the next week, most of Mason County stopped by Darlene's house to pay respects to her father and mother, the Senator and Mrs. Christmas. My family was among them, including me in little white gloves. We were there only briefly. People of our sort did not call on people of their sort. The length of our visit was timed to show we were aware of our station. I had to shake hands with Senator Christmas, Darlene and her brother Roger, who was eight, two years younger than we were, and then I had to kiss Mrs. Christmas, who leaned over and presented a cheek much smoother and more pampered than my mother's.

I can't ever remember not knowing Darlene Christmas. She and Mamie Todd and I were together from babyhood, when we were left in the church nursery during Sunday services. We started our schooling in the church kindergarten, where the teacher always asked Darlene to lead us in the morning prayer.

The next year we were enrolled in the private white-flight academy on the outskirts of town. The school's football field was named for Darlene's great-uncle, a former county attorney, and her father sat on the board of trustees.

In the sixth grade, the first year we elected class officers, Darlene ran for president. She was unopposed, although there were emotional contests for vice president, treasurer and secretary. Even in the sixth grade, we knew better than to challenge a Christmas. Darlene was our class president until we graduated.

I was friends off and on with Mamie. We were pals in the early grades, playing tag at recess and going to the same pajama parties. Sometimes I invited her on the family outings across the Lazy River to Stone Bridge for root beer floats.

Mamie didn't have much of a family life herself. Her father was a lawyer who died young of a heart attack, and her mother never seemed to recover from the shock of it. She was always nervous, pushing Mamie to excel in school and be popular with the boys.

Mamie and I drifted apart in our early teens. She was going to the school dances and meeting her dates at the ice cream parlor, and I wasn't interested, although at the time I didn't know why. We didn't become friends again until springtime in the tenth grade, when I was on the tennis team and she was the softball catcher. She had a car, and she used to give me a ride home after our practices.

Tenth grade was the year I found out I had a desire for girls.

A family named Darby moved into Mason County the summer before the school term started. The father was an ex-cop from New Jersey, brought in to run the security at a construction site where a new wing was being added to the hospital. The builder was having a lot of trouble with theft and suspected his workers were involved. He figured he could stop it if he imported a Yankee with no ties to the locals. It seemed to work.

The Darby family was Irish Catholic, which stood out in Mason County. There were six children, but only the youngest daughter was still living at home. Her name was Kim Darby, and she had dark Celtic features and not so much as a twitch of fat on her angular frame. Near the end of summer vacation I spotted her going into the post office, and my whole body started to quiver like a retriever on the hunt. Cupid's arrow was in me. For the first time in my life, I wished school would start so I could see her regularly.

Kim was in the eleventh grade, a year ahead of me. Immediately she was the talk of the academy, which didn't enroll many new students, let alone an Irish Catholic one. As if that wasn't enough, Kim turned out to be the best math student at the school, even better than the seniors, and she was a whiz with a hockey stick, playing goalie on the varsity team.

I didn't know what to call what I was feeling about her, but I was sure as hellfire and brimstone feeling it. Kim wasn't much of a talker or a mixer. I tried saying hello to her a few times, without much luck. She gave me the once-over and kept going.

I began attending the hockey games to see her. She could do magic in that goal cage, blocking the opposition with her pads and stick and kicks and back-against-the-wall glare. She had a look of disdain after she turned away the shots. On those rare occasions when she let a goal in, she turned the look on herself.

Kim won every game I watched. After the first two, I arranged to pass close to her.

"Nice going," I said, but all I got was the once-over again.

After the third game, I was stunned when the handshakes were finished on the field and she approached me.

"I've seen you hanging around," she said. "Do you want to come to my house?"

"When?"

"In the year two thousand. Now, you moron. What do you mean, when?"

"Sure. Now. OK," I stammered, blushing.

"All right. I have to take a quick shower, then I'll be out."

I waited, trembling with nervousness. I thought about her in the shower. I thought about her slender and soapy, with the silvery jets of water streaming across her young breasts. I tried not to think about them, but it was no use.

Her hair was still wet when she came outside, and the shower image stayed with me. I had to turn away, for fear she would see in my eyes what I was thinking.

"You played a good game," I said. It had been another shutout.

Kim shrugged. "The other team hardly took any shots on goal."

"They were afraid to. They knew you would stop them. They just kept passing to one another, hoping someone else would shoot."

We walked to her house, talking about the hockey game and school as we went. Her family was renting a place less than a mile from the academy. No one was home when we arrived.

"Where's your mother?" I asked.

"She had to take my father to the doctor after work. He hurt his back and can't drive. They won't be home until late."

Kim got us some Cokes from the refrigerator and invited me into her room. Even though we were alone, she closed the door.

"Did you ever play strip poker?" she asked.

"No."

"Do you want to?"

"Sure."

We sat on her bed to play. My stomach felt tight and my crotch was tingling. I was beginning to figure out what I was feeling. I wanted my clothes off. I desperately wanted to lose the game. I threw away good cards in my hand, trying not to be too obvious about it, but I think she knew.

Kim was naked to the waist when I lost the last hand and shed my panties. I stared at the cards, not knowing what to do.

"You're queer, aren't you?" she said.

"I don't know. I never thought about it. Maybe I am."

She came beside me, kissed me awkwardly on the lips, rubbed her palms across my breasts and stuck her hand between my legs. I shuddered from the sensations. She kissed me again, and then we got dressed.

We played strip poker throughout hockey season. Right before Christmas, the construction work at the hospital was completed, and Kim's family moved back to New Jersey. I never saw her again, but she left me knowing for sure what I was.

I had my eye on Mamie but kept my distance. I was content that she was agreeable to driving out to Stone Bridge weekends for root beer floats and to studying Latin together Thursday evenings before the weekly tests.

Amo, amas, amat. I love, you love, she loves. In the first verb we learned to conjugate, I found poetry in that dead language.

I switched from watching hockey to softball. Casually I studied Mamie in her catcher's crouch behind the plate, with the fabric of her uniform pulling smooth across her buttocks and her breasts locked away behind her chest protector, like a damsel in a dungeon.

I never approached her after the game. There always seemed to be some young man to take her arm and praise her play indulgently, as boys do when they see girls at sports. Often it was Collin, the tennis star, at her side, and the way she looked at him gave me no cause to disbelieve he was the reason she came to the tennis matches.

I admired her from afar, more afraid of revealing what I was than of being rejected. I could survive being spurned, but I dared not be exposed. How was

I to know that Mamie was having the same feelings and fears?

We walked in our parallel universes with little regret, finding it only natural. Repression was as much a part of life in Mason County as going to church and voting for Christmases.

There was one other passion besides girls that I discovered in the tenth grade. It was writing.

I had a magical teacher for English that year, an immigrant from England named Mrs. Cavendish, who could make words dance and charm them into telling stories. I fell under her spell, and she encouraged me. Her husband worked at the Mason County *Crier,* and she got him to ask the publisher, an old Christmas family retainer named Emily Frances Letard, whether I might be allowed at the newspaper as a sort of apprentice. Permission was granted.

The *Crier* was an afternoon publication, so the reporters showed up at daybreak to get their stories written before deadline. I went in with them and hung around the newsroom until I had to go to school. I fetched coffee, sharpened their pencils and filled their gluepots, and I knew where the half pint was hidden so I could bring them a swallow in a paper cup for doctoring their morning-after hangovers.

The building was an ancient, teeming place that trembled to its foundations when the presses lumbered to life. The newsroom itself was a ramshackle sanctum of unemptied ashtrays and cluttered desks. It ran on the jittery energy of clacking typewriters, fingered by reporters keeping one eye on their copy and the other on the clock and cursing.

The first morning I was there, I heard the editor bawling out his obituary clerk. "Winthrop! Let's put a little life in these obits!"

The second morning I saw the dean of the newsroom, a reporter named Robert E. Lee Travis, absent-mindedly drop his cigarette into his trash can while he was typing on deadline. The contents ignited without attracting Travis's attention, until the editor bellowed at him, "Robert E. Lee Travis! You're on fire!"

Travis never took his eyes off his copy. He dumped his coffee into the trash can and kept typing. The fire died out with a sibilant sigh.

I was quivering. Not only did I want to tell stories, I wanted to tell them there.

CHAPTER FOUR

I was retrieving a clip file of old newspaper stories for Robert E. Lee Travis from the morgue, when a copy boy named Steve tracked me down.

"Editor wants to see you," he said.

"Sweet Jesus. What did I do?"

"He didn't say."

"Was he mad?"

Steve gave me a look. "Have you ever seen him when he wasn't?"

I handed Steve the clips for Travis and walked across the newsroom toward the office of Arthur

Layton Calhoun, the editor of the Mason County *Crier*.

It was May of my senior year. I had put in more than two years of weekday mornings and occasional weekends at the newspaper, and my contacts with the editor had been limited to getting his coffee and staying out of his way. It was an arrangement I was very comfortable with. Arthur Layton Calhoun regarded human concourse as a necessary evil for getting the newspaper out. He rarely deviated from his philosophy of conversation: *If you can't say something nice about someone, say it loudly.*

Whatever was about to happen to me would happen in full view of the newsroom, because of the huge glass windows in the editor's office. Nor would anyone turn away if it got interesting. Gossip is not a sin in a newsroom. It's a way of life.

I was quaking as I paused at the open door. "Steve said you wanted to see me, Mr. Calhoun," I said, making sure I said Steve's name clearly. If this was Steve's idea of a prank, I wanted the blame up front where it belonged.

The editor didn't snarl. "You're the kid Cavendish recommended, aren't you?" he said.

"Yes, sir."

"It's about time for you to graduate, isn't it?"

"Yes, sir, in three weeks."

"What are you doing afterwards?"

"I'll be attending State University in the fall."

"What are you studying?"

"Well, I hope to take journalism," I said and blushed, sure that he would find it presumptuous of me.

Calhoun grunted. It was a negative grunt, I was

certain, and I dearly wanted to flee. This had to be it. The editor of the Mason County *Crier* was about to tell me I didn't belong in newspaper.

"Don't waste your time," he said, mortifying me so much I almost missed what came next. "Take English. Take history. Take political science. Take anything but those wimp journalism courses. College can't teach you newspapering. You have to learn it on the job."

"Yes, sir!"

"Now what are you doing this summer?"

"I don't rightly know, sir. My mother was going to ask about some part-time work at the library for me."

"Well, listen. I'm taking Winthrop off obits for the summer. I'm using him on general assignment to fill in for reporters on vacation. How would you like to be Winthrop's summer replacement?"

I was stunned. By all rights, the copy boys should be in line for the obituary clerk's job, and here I was leapfrogging past them. I wasn't even a boy. Girls almost never got a chance in newspaper.

"I can't pay you much, but it will probably be more than you'd make at the library," Calhoun said.

He squinted. I surmised he was calculating how little he could get away with offering me, but I didn't care.

"I'd love to work here, Mr. Calhoun," I said.

Graduation was held on a sweltering evening on the Charles Shelby Christmas Memorial Field at the academy. It was timed to end before the birds stopped twittering and the mosquitoes came out.

We graduates were drilled to step in time to the band's solemn rendition of *Pomp and Circumstance* for the processional, but the turf was soggy from the early summer rains and sucked at the high heels of the girls' white shoes. It turned our march into more of a stutter.

The girls wore white gowns, chastely hemmed at mid-calf, and the boys wore black. Beneath those robes we sweated through our best dresses and Sunday suits.

We were marshaled roughly by size, small to tall, which was fine with me, because it put me next to Mamie. Darlene was the last of the girls.

We had the customary Christmas program. Darlene was the valedictorian, and her father, Senator Christmas, was the keynote speaker. In complementary upbeat speeches, they told us we were leaving our collective past to embark on our separate destinies.

It seemed so at the time. I had my summer job at the *Crier,* and then I was off to State University to study anything but journalism so I could make it in newspaper. Mamie was doing office work for the summer at her late father's law firm and then was taking pre-law at Duke University. Darlene was spending the summer as an intern in her father's Senate office, before enrolling at Radcliffe. She intended to pursue a career in politics, which she called "public service."

Little did we know, our destinies were about as separate as fingers on a hand.

CHAPTER FIVE

The obituary clerk's job was the most terrifying work I ever did.

You had to call up the newly bereaved and confirm the departure of the dearly beloved, and then you had to go over the list of the next of kin that the funeral parlor provided and make sure it was complete with the names spelled right, and then you had to coax out little details about the deceased so the obituaries wouldn't all read so drearily the same. It was amazing how many families, after spending a lifetime with the late lamented, could only remember them as devoted mothers, loving husbands and faithful churchgoers.

I learned to ask — sorrowfully, of course — about pets left behind, hobbies, even favorite songs that would be played at the service. It was dreadful work, staying on the phone with the mourners, but the sooner you hung up to quiet your nerves, the more likely you were to write obits that bored Mr. Calhoun.

Calhoun read every obit. He considered them a specialty of the *Crier*. He printed them inside somber black borders with angels in the upper corners, and he ran them when possible with recent photos, which were the obit clerk's responsibility to cajole out of the grieving family.

Calhoun wanted the obituaries tasteful, and he wanted them right. It was not easy to write little meaningful stories about the dearly departed, when everyone reading them knew more about the deceased than you did and didn't mind letting the editor know.

I never forgot the day Calhoun came lumbering out of his office and made right for Winthrop. The poor clerk had noted the deceased was a member of the Victory Gospel Baptist Church choir but had gotten his voice section wrong.

"Winthrop! Do you know what the difference is between baritone and bass? About two hundred fifty churchgoing readers, that's what!"

I became a crack obit clerk, inspired by my fear of Calhoun. My reward was that he ignored me throughout the summer. We didn't speak until the week before I left for State University, when he summoned me to his office.

"I can use you again next summer," Calhoun said, "maybe even work you in for a little general assignment."

The week before Labor Day, I drove out to Stone Bridge with Mamie for one last root beer float, said good-bye to my folks and hopped a northbound bus for State University.

I was seventeen. I felt free. I felt anonymous. I could reinvent myself any way I wanted.

State University was a campus of muddy-red brick buildings and white columns, vivid green swards criss-crossed by dark clay footpaths and overhung with lofty trees drooping Spanish moss. A carillon played the introductory bars of "Dixie" every day at noon.

State University attracted families like mine, the shabby genteel whose riches and reputation had petered out a generation or so ago, leaving only the pretensions. There also were a sprinkling of Yankees, harboring romantic but misguided notions of the South, and the occasional scion of a prominent family, recently expelled from a finer institution for academic or social infractions but accepted at State, no questions asked.

The college was located in the state capital, with its classrooms and dormitories adjacent to the Statehouse and a short walk from the governor's mansion. It was the primary reason the capital routinely was cited as one of the prettiest in the country.

The governor and the legislators held season passes to the football games, where they hooted and hollered like fraternity brothers, and sometimes a congressman or two came along. During budget season, the university president invited the chairmen of the Senate Finance Committee and the House Appropriations Committee to sit in his personal box. At other times, the invitations were rotated. Once there was a photo in the university newspaper of the president in his box with Senator Christmas.

I did what Mr. Calhoun advised, enrolling in English and history and political science courses. I steered clear of the sororities, even though they had the choicest housing selection. I didn't favor their collective lifestyle, and I didn't want them prying into mine.

I resurrected my habit of attending women's sports. In volleyball season I got lucky.

The best player on the varsity team was a blonde lefthander nicknamed "Spike." I was smitten from the first moment of the season opener. Spike arched to serve, her breasts lifted and she smashed a wicked slam through the opposition. One to nothing, State.

Spike was a team player, but she dominated the court, setting the ball, spiking at the net, running off a streak of winning serves. I admired the smooth calves, the sure hands and the graceful line of the shoulders, but I fell for the smile. It was never cocky, and it never went away. It was a beacon of encouragement to her teammates, as well as an acknowledgment of her own athletic talents.

I was bold and approached her after State won the match on her serve.

"Congratulations. You're a mighty fine player," I said.

"Thank you."

"My name's Jess Marceau."

"Lucinda St. James. But everybody calls me Spike."

"No wonder."

"What? You don't think Lucinda's a nice name?"

"No. I saw you spike."

She laughed and offered me her hand. It was calloused. She withdrew it to wipe the sweat from her forehead and self-consciously run it through her tousled curls. Her eyes were dark as a deer's.

"Do you play sports?" Spike asked.

"A little tennis. I'm more the academic type. I write for a newspaper."

"The university paper?"

"No. The Mason County *Crier,* back in my hometown."

"Oh! That sounds exciting. Do you get bylines?"

"Not yet. I spent the summer writing obits. Mr. Calhoun, the editor, won't let us cover the living until we've practiced on the dead."

Spike laughed again. "Listen, I have to go. The team is meeting for pizza. Will you come to the next match? It's on Tuesday."

"Thank you kindly. I'd love to."

We began courting. I went to her volleyball games, and she read my papers for Creative Writing. We studied together at the library and found an ice cream parlor that dispensed passable root beer floats.

Spike was a junior, two years ahead of me. She wanted to be a phys ed teacher and certainly had the credentials. Before she graduated, I watched her pitch for the softball team and run a blistering cross country, in addition to the volleyball matches that inspired her nickname.

Spike came from Jefferson County in the northern part of the state. She was descended from a Confederate captain who had fallen at Gettysburg, fighting for the secessionist side that omitted itself from Mr. Lincoln's address by dying in vain.

Spike had two younger brothers, twins, still in high school. They made All-American in football in the fall and were on their way to doing the same in basketball. Every college in the country was madly recruiting Terry and Jerry St. James, but they were blind to the inducements. They had their twin hearts set on the Citadel, where it was still an article of faith that the South would rise again.

In the spring, with the air fragrant from thousands and thousands of new blooms, I found my courage one evening as we left the library for the dormitories. I told Spike about Kim Darby and the strip poker games. She was silent afterwards, and I feared I had made a dreadful mistake. Then she explained she was involved with a woman who had graduated last year. They were writing, but lately the letters were dwindling, and she didn't feel there was much left.

Spike's roommate was leaving for the weekend. We made plans to use her room.

After classes on Friday afternoon, I went to her dormitory. The halls were cheerful bedlam, as students collected their luggage for a two-day escape or debated which campus parties to attend. They arranged rides, swapped clothes and gossiped about their dates. In about an hour, nearly everyone was gone.

It was the Seventies, and the university had a rule that a girl couldn't have a boy in her room with the door closed, but it didn't have one about us.

"It's a good thing you're a girl, or I couldn't close the door," Spike said.

"If I wasn't a girl, you wouldn't even want to."

Spike had spruced up the room with a dish of lavender water, and ever after I never could understand why people said it reminded them of old ladies. To me it was the scent of love.

There was no sense pretending we were there for anything other than what we were there for. Spike took my hand and brought me to her bed, laid me back against the pillows and kissed me.

What a kiss it was. This was no Kim Darby kiss, a brush against the mouth with unmelting lips. This was flowers and honey, blue sky and waterfalls, a soft, yielding touch that transported me and resonated like chimes all through my body.

"I didn't know what I've been missing," I said when I finally came up for air.

"Jess, darlin', that's just the beginning."

Spike showed me all sorts of things you can do with your hands and your mouth and the sensation of body against body. When you are eighteen and twenty years old, you can do a lot.

By the time we lay sweaty and giggling in our sin and satisfaction, the night had closed in on us. Spike half-raised herself to pull back the curtain, and we watched the dark and eternal theater of fireflies and other winged creatures in the chirp and buzz and dart of survival. Moths beat a fluttery assault against the glowing lampposts of the capital.

As she stretched to hold the curtain, I stroked her breast with my knuckles. After a moment she let the curtain go. I lay back and she gazed at me, making love once again with her eyes.

My college transcript shows that I must have studied, because I made the dean's list that spring, but all I remember is Spike.

Spike and me in her room when her roommate was away. Spike and me in my room during a break between classes. Spike and me in the library with her knee casually touching mine. Spike and me in a borrowed car driving to an overgrown dirt road. Spike and me at the movies sharing an armrest. Spike and me spooning and sipping suggestively through root beer floats. Spike stealing a key to the towel room at the women's gym for some privacy when we were desperate.

We parted reluctantly when the term ended. Spike left for Jefferson County, and I went back to Mason County and the *Crier*.

I wrote obituaries and got my first byline — a story on the volunteer fire station acquiring a dalmatian pup for a mascot. It ran on the local page with a photo of Senator Christmas petting the dog while the company of firefighters looked on. Mrs. Cavendish, my old English teacher, telephoned her congratulations. I mailed a copy of the newspaper to Spike.

Not a week later, I feared I was about to get my second byline. Senator Christmas's elderly aunt broke her hip and died while convalescing. I was scared to death I would be assigned the obituary, but Calhoun gave it to an experienced reporter, one favored by the Christmas family.

Not much else happened that summer. Mamie Todd was in town, but she was dating a young associate at the law firm and I hardly saw her. Darlene Christmas was in Europe.

I counted the days until I could return to college and Spike.

CHAPTER SIX

I don't think I ever really fell in love with Spike. Perhaps it was because Mamie was still in the back of my mind. Perhaps it was because I knew it could never last, not in the South, not then.

We simply lacked the resourcefulness to stay together, to weave the web of excuses it would take. Instead, Spike returned to Jefferson County with her degree in physical education, and I remained at State College. Before her graduation, we did escape to the coast, choosing a shabby little resort town that had gone out of fashion a generation ago. The motel proprietor was grateful for the business and asked no questions, and we laughed and loved through a torrid weekend. We parted as friends, without tears.

After Spike left, I reverted to my habit of haunting women's sporting events, and although I saw many fine games of hockey, volleyball, softball and tennis and admired the form and grace of several archers, I did not find companionship.

Well, I had other ways to pass the time. I took to wandering into the Statehouse, but to my naive surprise, there were no James Madisons or Jefferson Davises debating the great issues of the day. I was stunned to find ordinary, even petty men occupying the stuffy chambers and doing the bidding of the moneyed interests that had bought and paid for them — timber lords and agribusinessmen with plantation-size tracts, bankers and lawyers and owners of textile mills. The lobbyists circulated on the very floor of the houses, and the legislators who passed me in the gilt hallways often had a hitch in their walk and whiskey on their breath.

The spectacle was as shocking as it was irresistible. I wondered what fantasyland my political science professors lived in, with their quaint fictions of how a bill becomes a law unsullied by the reek and glitter of earthly rewards.

One day in early spring, when a rain as fine as spray perfume washed out the women's softball game, I walked to the Statehouse for diversion. I was scanning a list of committee meetings when I heard someone call me.

It was Roger Christmas, Darlene's little brother. He was dolled up like a junior legislator, pinstripe suit and French cuffs, but his blond hair fell on his forehead and his eyes showed the suffering of a boy at church.

I was surprised to see him. The last I had heard about Roger, he was headed to New Hampshire for Dartmouth College.

"Roger Christmas, as I live and breathe! What are you doing here? It's a little early for spring break, isn't it?"

The suffering spread from his eyes to an ironic smile. "I'm not on spring break. It's still the dead of winter up there and everything is stone cold — the ground, the weather, the snow, the buildings and the people. Especially the people. Jess, I quit the school. I just couldn't abide all those Yankees."

"What was the matter?"

"They're not like us. They blink too much and they talk too fast, they go to Presbyterian churches, and they've never had grits. A praline would freeze in their mouths from the chill."

"Well, why did you go there in the first place?"

Roger's shoulders drooped. "Father sent me. He said I would become more cosmopolitan if I was educated in the North. But I finally convinced him how miserable I was, and he said I could come home if I worked in his Senate office for the rest of the semester."

"How long have you been here?"

"Since last week. I hate this, too, all these people kissing up to me because I'm Senator Christmas's son, but at least it won't be for too long. Father says I have to go back to school in the fall. He wants to send me to one of those Quaker schools in

Philadelphia, but I swear, I'm holding out for someplace sane like Vanderbilt. If I can't stay in the South, I'll die."

Roger was making me nervous. I had never talked to a Christmas, not even Darlene, for this long, and I certainly hadn't been privy to family matters.

"Anyway, Jess, what are you doing here?"

I told him, and he laughed ruefully. "If you're so fascinated with the legislature, maybe you should be working in Father's office."

He startled me by taking my hand. "It's so nice to see someone from Mason County! Can I buy you a cup of coffee and some pie?"

"Thank you kindly, Roger, but no. I don't want to take you away from your responsibilities."

He shrugged. "It's a slow day. Father's got a bill on the floor tomorrow, so he's off with the lobbyists from both sides. It'll be my pleasure."

I thought he would take me to the coffee shop downstairs, but he escorted me outside to The General, an inn and restaurant across the street. It was the fanciest place in the capital and simultaneously the most public and the most discreet. The knowing staff could give you a table so everyone could spy you socializing with the lieutenant governor, or else hide you and your companions from the most prying of eyes. Its starch and polish had me thoroughly intimidated.

The bell captain touched his cap and wished Roger a good afternoon, and the headwaiter said, "I'll show you to Senator Christmas's table."

We were seated about three-quarters of the way back, not quite so far as the tables reserved for the governor and the lieutenant governor and the chairmen of the Senate Finance and House Appropriations Committees, but within conversational distance of them.

Darlene Christmas would have preened to be there, but Roger did all he could to take it in stride. I understood he wasn't showing off but simply trying to be nice to me.

We had coffee with the sweetest cream I ever tasted and pecan pie that Roger said was the best in the state, if not the entire South. We marveled over it together and gossiped about the people we knew back home in Mason County. Then Roger dunked his cuff in his coffee while reaching for the sugar, and the waiter came hurrying with a napkin to sop it up, and we laughed and laughed and discovered we liked each other.

"Let's do this again," Roger said.

"That will be fine by me."

I saw quite a bit of Roger Christmas that spring semester in the state capital. He often talked earnestly about his future, how he wanted to be a lawyer but didn't want to go into politics.

"What does your father say about that?"

"I haven't told him."

"Are you going to?"

"Maybe I won't have to. By the time it becomes necessary, I expect Darlene will be more than able to carry on the family tradition. She has a way of persuading Father to her point of view."

"You're a reluctant Christmas, aren't you?"

Roger's smile was rueful and affectionate. "Jess, sometimes you understand me better than I do."

When the semester ended, I returned home for another stint at the Mason County *Crier*. Roger, after winning his argument with his father, went off to Vanderbilt for summer session to make up the credits he had missed.

I didn't encounter Roger again for a few years. When I did, it changed my life.

CHAPTER SEVEN

Mamie and I were situated on the porch of her house, enjoying the light nighttime breezes that swept out the cloying heat and mustiness of the day. Moths beat mindlessly against the screens, like a display of tiny flying feathers and dark jewels. The flickering lanterns of the fireflies were as random as the bellowing of the bullfrogs was rhythmic.

Even in the darkest of my days, I had loved the South at night, when it stirred and stretched and gave in to the secret yearnings that it despaired of quenching in the torpid light. It would rise again, after it slept awhile. It would.

"I never knew you got to know Roger Christmas so well," Mamie said.

"That's not the half of it," I replied.

Mamie sat on a glider, and I lay with my head in her lap while she tousled my hair and rocked us with a foot against a low table disarrayed by beer bottles and empty coffee cups.

"My jaw hurts from talking. I haven't strung so many sentences together since I left town," I said.

"It's late. We can talk more tomorrow."

I looked out at the night, savoring its twitch and hum. "Do you know what I've always wanted to do?"

"What?"

"Make love someplace where you won't be discovered but you could be."

"You mean, like here?"

"I mean, like here."

Mamie's skin was as pale as the moon above us and just as bewitching. I was half-crazed as she lay exposed on the open porch.

There is nothing quite like a fantasy brought to life. She was yielding and tender, and I was afire, driven to an arousal I scarcely felt possible. The glider swayed beneath us, and I lost myself in her curves and swells and pockets and our mutual exploration of delight.

You can go to the heights of passion when you are excited, or you can go to the depths of passion when you are thoroughly satisfied, but in this rapture I was tossed and plunged from one to the other until I could move no more.

"Darlin'," Mamie whispered, "it has never ever been like this. Never ever."

We fell asleep there, naked on the glider, as innocent and unselfconscious as babies, until the songbirds woke us at first light and we scrambled inside, laughing, before the milkman came by.

Mamie asked me to go to the cafe with her, so I did, dressed in the blue shirt she bought me and my faded jeans. I made myself useful by washing dishes in the back while she chatted with her customers and presided over the cash register.

About noon, when the lunchtime crowd was building, the telephone rang. Mamie took the call and then beckoned me over.

"I've had new menus printed at Slaughter's, and they're ready. Do you think you could collect them for me?"

"Slaughter's?"

"Yes, you know. It's by the bank downtown in Mason City, where it's always been."

I did remember it. Slaughter's was a cluttered print shop, defiantly ramshackle, in the otherwise neat center of town. No one bothered Slaughter, though, because he printed the Christmas campaign fliers at cost and refused the business of the occasional challengers, forcing them to truck to another county for their brochures. Every now and then, if they complained to the State Election Bureau, he would print their leaflets, but he always made mistakes.

Slaughter's was next to the Mason County Commercial Trust, where my father had worked, and across the way from the county courthouse, the hub of the Christmas empire where Darlene now occupied the office.

"Slaughter's," I said again, stalling. I hadn't decided exactly when I wanted to cross the Lazy River into Mason County, and here Mamie was asking me to do it. Well, maybe that was the best way. Don't make a bigger deal out of it than it was. "Sure. Where are your car keys?"

The miracle was that I still had a driver's license, although the address on it was many towns ago. I had kept it because I feared the hassle of reapplying, if I let it lapse and then needed to renew. Ex-cons are not enthusiastic about meeting up with anyone wearing a badge.

The ten-mile drive between Stone Bridge and Mason City once had seemed like an eternity to me, when I was a child sitting in the back seat and thirsting for a root beer float. Now it was a short drop to hell, no more than the jerk of a hangman's noose, and I was there.

I did not look around. I did not glance at the courthouse to see whether the same old souls as always were sitting there until the afternoon sun struck them and they switched to the shade of the barber shop across the street. I did not want to see that nothing had changed, that life here had the sameness of a jail cell to it, which is what it was and what it represented to me.

There were several dusty parking spaces right in front of Slaughter's, and I pulled in gratefully and hurried inside. The clerk looked to be a kid barely out of high school, no one that I recognized, and in moments I was on my way.

I blinked in the sunlight and then froze, as a

voice that was too familiar called my name. I was suddenly as immobile as Lot's wife, turned to a pillar of salt in her futile endeavor to escape from the cities of sin.

"Jess Marceau! Have you come back?"

It was the hoarse cackle of Quinton Coombs, the secretary to two generations of Christmases. He was Darlene's chief aide, as he had been for her father, and I should have known he would spot me. He had been the eyes and ears of the family for a very long time.

"Hello, Mr. Coombs," I said softly.

"What are you doing here, Jess Marceau?"

"I came to pay my respects to my parents' graves. It's been a long time," I lied, and he knew it.

"What does that have to do with Slaughter's print shop?" He glanced at the package I held, but the menus were wrapped in plain brown paper that gave no clues.

"Nothing. This is just an errand."

"We didn't expect you to come back here. I'm sure Senator will be very interested to hear about your return."

"Yes, sir. I was just going."

I dared not look at him again, but I'm sure he watched me get into Mamie's car and took notice of the license plate. I was mindful to stay within the speed limit as I drove back.

Mamie looked concerned when I told her about Quinton Coombs. "It's almost as though they've been lying in wait for you, all these years. I expect Coombs went straight into Slaughter's to find out what you were doing," she said.

"For sure. Between that and the tag on the Ford,

I'm sure he's put us together and told Senator," I said.

"They'll be plotting already."

"I don't much like the sound of that."

"We know what they're capable of," Mamie said.

When the workday was over, Mamie and I returned to her house with some sense of urgency. We rushed through dinner and settled down on the porch, so I could resume the tale of what happened after I got my degree from State and Mr. Calhoun gave me a job at the *Crier.*

Robert E. Lee Travis was known to expound scornfully on the difference between a reporter and a journalist: "A journalist is a reporter who can afford to wear a suit."

Mr. Calhoun didn't pay anyone enough to be a journalist, not even Robert E. Lee Travis. When I started out, I had to move back home with my folks and borrow money from them for some decent clothes.

Still, I was a newspaperwoman. I had a press card, and the people in the newsroom called me gruffly by my last name, and the copy boys brought me coffee, which I learned to drink black, because you never knew when the cream turned sour or what manner of vermin had crawled into the sugar.

Mr. Calhoun handed out the daily assignments, writing them down longhand in a large canvas-colored assignment book that memorialized what we did from January 1 to December 31 each year. He started me out with meetings of the ladies' garden club, reviews of school plays, interviews with visiting ministers and grand openings of new stores. I yearned to cover county commissioners' sessions and political meetings, but I was content to wait my turn.

I was so bored with the reporting that I learned to find joy in the writing. I developed a reputation for fine word pictures, but I was more of an illustrator than an artist. Creativity wasn't particularly prized in newspaper work in Mason County, where people liked things as they always were and expected the paper to help them stay the same.

I got a promotion to court reporter and became skilled at describing murder, rape and other forms of mayhem in ways that balanced delicacy and titillation. I think it came from all those summers of gilding death for the obituaries.

I saved enough money to move into a small apartment, downtown in Mason City within walking distance of the *Crier.*

Meanwhile, Mamie got a law degree from Duke and came home to a job in the county attorney's office. Darlene Christmas took her law degree from Harvard and was hired as assistant legal counsel to the Mason County Democratic Party.

I saw both of them with some frequency around the county courthouse, and sometimes Mamie and I would have a cup of coffee together. My heart beat, but I had professional obligations and kept my distance. Occasionally Mamie assisted a senior prosecutor on a case I covered. She often praised my stories, and I wondered whether she knew why I blushed so badly.

The courthouse was always a buzz of activity, but

it was busiest in election years, especially when Senator Christmas was on the ballot. He was up this time, and old Quinton Coombs shuttled almost hourly to the election commissioner's office. Often Darlene was with him.

Roger Christmas, who was taking his time getting through Vanderbilt, came home to work for his father's campaign. He smiled warmly whenever he saw me, but the conditions had changed around us, and we didn't dare socialize.

This particular election was unusual. There was a real candidate on the ballot opposing Senator Christmas, in addition to the customary crazies and perennial losers whose names always appeared. This time the county sheriff was running against Senator Christmas, because Senator Christmas was running a candidate against him.

There had been a falling-out some time back, when the senator came to believe that Sheriff Mickey Lemay had forgotten just who put him on the ballot in the first place. Senator Christmas was backing a new candidate for sheriff, and Mickey Lemay knew his chances of beating the senator's man were about as good as Confederate war bonds. Rather than suffer the humiliation, Lemay announced for the senator's seat.

Lemay couldn't win, but he had enough of a name and a following to make a pest of himself.

The primary was scheduled for the last Saturday in June. I was following all this from afar until the Wednesday before the voting.

It was a sweltering summer night, and I was having trouble sleeping. Then my telephone rang, and the world turned upside down.

The call began in a whisper. "Hello, Jess? This is Roger Christmas."

"Roger! Is something the matter?"

"I can't talk too loud, and I might have to hang up on you. We've just had a terrible family row. Father came home early from campaigning, said he wasn't feeling well and went to bed. When Mother tried to wake him for supper, he was dead."

"Oh, Roger! I'm so sorry."

"That's not the worst of it. Mother and Darlene want to keep his death a secret until after the primary on Saturday. They expect he can get more than fifty percent of the vote, which would guarantee he's the only candidate for the general election. Then they can get the governor to appoint Darlene to take his place."

Roger's voice wavered, and I wondered whether he would sob, but he got himself under control and went on. "Jess, I think it's monstrous. It's disrespectful to Father to treat him this way. He deserves to be laid to rest honorably, without politics getting in the way. If it means the family has to lose the Senate seat, then so be it."

"Roger, that's horrible. What can I do to help you?"

"You work for the *Crier,* don't you?"

Oh, my God. Until Roger spoke the words, I thought he was calling me as an old friend, not a reporter. I wasn't nearly experienced enough to handle this.

"Listen, Jess. Obviously you can't quote me, or I'll be drummed out of the family forever. But there is a way you can get this. Hiram Broadbent, the undertaker, is on his way over now to attend to

Father right here. He's been sworn to secrecy, but he's not happy about it. I expect you could find out from him. I dare not talk any longer. Good luck."

I was shaking as I hung up the phone. Reporters are supposed to dream of this — the call in the night that leads to the story of a lifetime — but it wasn't a dream, it was a nightmare.

What was I supposed to do? How could I go up against the Christmas family when Roger himself was afraid to?

I needed help. I dialed Mr. Calhoun, even though the thought of waking him was nearly as frightening as dealing with the Christmases.

"Mr. Calhoun, this is Jess Marceau. I'm terribly sorry to wake you, but I just got this tip . . ."

He didn't yell. He listened silently and then asked, "Who told you?"

"I really shouldn't say."

Calhoun groaned at that but didn't press me. "You're sure this is from a good source?"

"The best."

"I was afraid of that." He paused, and I could hear him sucking in air. "All right. We'll do what we have to do. I'll pick you up in ten minutes at your place, and we'll drive over to the Christmases. If we're wrong, there will be hell to pay. If we're right, it will be even worse."

Calhoun and I drove to the Christmases' neighborhood. Despite their unequaled standing in the county, they had never put on airs. They still lived inside the Mason City limits on a dignified street, where ancient trees provided shade and serenity, and the bankers, lawyers and other favored citizens who lived there respected one another's privacy. It would not have occurred to the Christmases to move into one of those pretentious houses erected near the new country club outside of town, to hobnob with the timber lords and textile kings and other nouveau riche who were attracted, fat and fickle as summer moths, to the South after Lee surrendered at Appomattox.

Calhoun parked at the end of the street, and we walked in, stopping at a hedge that screened us in the darkness from the Christmas house. It was the only residence with lights burning. The undertaker's black Cadillac sat across the street.

"We wait," Calhoun muttered. He double-checked the camera he had brought along.

We sweated, swatted mosquitoes and listened to our wristwatches tick. It was tense enough to make my muscles twitch, and I couldn't ever remember the night air feeling so thick. If Mr. Broadbent didn't come out soon, I was going to drown like a fish, open-mouthed and flopping, in this muggy darkness.

Eventually the door opened, and the undertaker walked out. Calhoun squeezed off some photos and then handed the camera to me. "Stay here," he said.

He walked briskly toward the house, intercepting the undertaker just as he got to his car.

"Hello, Hiram," Calhoun said.

Mr. Broadbent gave him a long look. "Hello, Arthur," he said.

"What brings you out here, Hiram?"

"A man could ask you the same question."

"I came to see you."

"Are you sticking your nose into my business for personal or professional reasons, Arthur?"

"Professional, Hiram."

"I'll be going along then."

"Has Senator Christmas passed on, Hiram?"

"Now, Arthur, you know I can't answer that."

"It seems to me, Hiram, that an undertaker who knowingly breaks the state law on timely burials would be in danger of losing his license."

"Who says I'm breaking the law?"

"Certainly not I, but I might have to rethink my position in a day or two."

"Are you threatening me?"

"Perish the thought, Hiram. I'm just trying to get my question answered."

"And I told you, I couldn't." Mr. Broadbent stared off into the night for a moment, then said, "I'll tell you this, Arthur. I've been in this business a long time. I started helping my father, God rest his soul, lay out the dead when I was four. I learned to knot a necktie by doing theirs. In all those years, this is the first time I've ever made a house call, and I hope to high heaven I never have to do it again."

Sharply at eight o'clock in the morning, Mr. Calhoun and I gathered at the desk of Ellis Witby, the *Crier*'s political writer. Ellis phoned Senator Christmas's office and asked to speak with him. Quinton Coombs came on the line, and Ellis scrawled Coombs' replies on a yellow legal pad so Calhoun and I could follow the conversation.

"Good morning, Mr. Coombs, this is Ellis Witby at the *Crier*. I'm doing an election roundup, and I need to talk to Senator Christmas."

"He's not in. Maybe I can help you," Coombs said.

"Thank you kindly, Mr. Coombs, but the primary is only three days away, and my assignment is to get comments from him on how he likes his chances."

"He likes them fine. You've been around a long time, Ellis, you can smell victory as well as we can. I predict better than fifty percent."

"When can I talk to Senator Christmas?"

"Not today."

"But, Mr. Coombs —"

"I said, *not today*."

"Mr. Coombs, is Senator Christmas dead?"

"What sort of a sensational, yellow-journalism question is that? Does your publisher know what you're doing?"

"Mr. Coombs, what was Mr. Broadbent doing at the Christmas house around midnight last night?"

Ellis tapped his pencil on the legal pad through a considerable silence. Finally he wrote, "The family is shocked and grief-stricken. We are trying to pull together a statement in this most difficult of times. The family has a right to its dignity and privacy and to be spared the sort of intrusion that you personally are forcing upon the Christmases right now."

"I'm very sorry, Mr. Coombs, but we're putting a newspaper to bed with this story at noon today, with or without a statement from the family. I'll be waiting for your call."

The sweat was dripping from Ellis's forehead onto

the legal pad. Calhoun and I were in the same state. For three people who had just cracked a blockbuster of a story, we were as grim as could be.

"I suspect Coombs will be calling the publisher," Ellis said.

"I know it," Calhoun replied. "You two start writing the main story. I'll get Grandy working on an account of the Senator's life and have photo develop the pictures I took last night. If we get a statement from the family, we'll run it in full. I'll be in with Mrs. Letard."

The newsboys could have hawked Thursday's paper for five dollars a pop, they went so fast. This was no tasteful account of death with the black borders and the angels that Mr. Calhoun normally prided himself on. This was journalism in the raw, an assault on all who came in contact with it, the readers and writers and the people it was about.

The *Crier* by nature shied away from this sort of story. We did not rip the fabric of society, we mended it. But not this time.

A headline screamed: *Senator Christmas Dead.* Underneath came the story, written by Ellis Witby and me. It began this way:

> *State Sen. Orrin Emmett Christmas, the most powerful elected official that Mason County has ever known, died suddenly in his sleep last evening, throwing Saturday's primary election into chaos.*
>
> *This untimely death wasn't announced by*

the Christmas family until mid-morning today, after the senator's office was questioned about it by the Crier, *which learned of it late last night from an anonymous caller.*

The Christmas family denied it had considered covering up the death until the polls closed . . .

Mr. Calhoun stared at one of the first papers off the presses. "Let's hope we all have jobs tomorrow," he said.

CHAPTER EIGHT

When Sheriff Mickey Lemay heard that Senator Christmas was dead, he did a little dance in the back room of the local post of the Veterans of Foreign Wars.

"I'm going to the legislature, boys," he giggled.

The sheriff's high-stepping was premature. Senator Christmas hadn't spent a lifetime building up his power to have it stopped by something as mundane as death.

Even as Lemay danced, the Central Committee of

the State Democratic Party was convening an emergency session in the capital. At the governor's request, the Central Committee was to determine its role and responsibilities in preserving the integrity of the Mason County senatorial primary.

Someone found a clause in the bylaws that said the party had a duty to fill a vacancy on the ballot by inserting a candidate acceptable to the members of the Central Committee. Up until now, this clause was invoked only for general elections when there otherwise would be no Democratic candidate on the ballot. It had never been used for primaries, when there was a whole host of Democrats to compete legitimately for the nomination, but there was always a first time.

The Central Committee declared that Senator Christmas's death had created a vacancy on the ballot. It further declared that the vacancy would be filled by the late senator's daughter Darlene.

Mickey Lemay howled bloody murder when he found out what the Central Committee had done, and he decided to sue. No Mason County lawyer would take his case, though, so he had to hire one from across the Lazy River in Stone Bridge. The lawyer, who was nobody's fool, charged Lemay an astronomical fee and made sure everyone knew it. Word was leaked to Ellis Witby, and the *Crier* ran a front-page story that left all of Mason County delightedly shocked and snickering.

Lemay and his attorney went to court. Even though the case was heard in the Mason County Courthouse where I covered all legal matters, another reporter was assigned in my place. I went anyway, as did nearly anyone else who could find the time. Mamie was there, squeezed against the back wall with other assistant county attorneys. The Christmases, who were in mourning, did not attend.

It took the judge seventeen minutes from *oyez* to gavel to throw the case out. Unlike Mickey Lemay, the judge hadn't forgotten who put him on the bench in the first place.

When Senator Christmas was laid to rest, the ceremony was part funeral and part political debut for Darlene. Her mother stood on one side of her and the governor stood on the other, and between the two of them, they introduced Darlene to everyone.

Darlene wore a smart black suit, purchased especially for the occasion, but easily as appropriate for the Senate chamber as a funeral. She accepted condolences solemnly and listened sharply as her mother and the governor advised her of the social and political pedigree of the mourners, whose attitudes ranged from sympathetic to deferential, depending upon their places in the hierarchy. The torch was passing.

The receiving line alone took four hours. The Central Baptist Church was the biggest in Mason County, but it had no more chance of accommodating all the mourners than of hosting the World Series.

Quinton Coombs stood at the doorway, granting admission to those worthy of seating and directing the rest into the churchyard. The governor and lieutenant governor were inside, as were Cabinet secretaries, almost the entire legislature, judges and county officials. Mrs. Letard, the *Crier* publisher, was shown to a pew up front.

The heat was perishing. The church windows were wide open, with everyone inside praying futilely for even a whisper of a breeze. The jam of people outside were a damp and wilting mass as they pressed forward to try to see and hear.

Senator Christmas, a waxy image with hands molded piously on his chest and his countenance fixed heavenward, lay in his coffin. So many floral arrangements crowded upon him that he appeared to be floating on a flowery sea.

The preacher, Armand Dupree, knew an opportunity when he saw one. His eulogy lasted nearly an hour, his voice rolling over the assemblage in booming cadences. He grieved over the senator's death, gave thanks for the senator's life and was gratified afterwards when Quinton Coombs whispered that his offer to serve as the Senate chaplain would be looked upon favorably.

I loitered through the funeral at the fringes of the crowd. From the reception I got, I thought I was the ghost and not Senator Christmas. No one wanted to have anything to do with a reporter who helped to break an unauthorized story about the senator's death.

After the dirt was heaped atop the grave and the last prayers uttered, I was one of the last to leave the churchyard. The sun was slanting toward the horizon, its blinding rays piling another plague of misery upon the scorching heat, when I felt a hand touch my shoulder. It was so gentle that I had a momentary sense of coolness.

Roger Christmas had found me. He smiled sadly and said, "It was a brave thing you did."

"I'm just now finding that out. I didn't know at the time, or perhaps I wouldn't have done it."

"Yes, around these parts they shoot the messenger."

Senator Christmas died on a Wednesday evening. The *Crier* broke the story in Thursday afternoon's edition. The Central Committee of the State Democratic Party met Thursday night and put Darlene on the ballot, and Sheriff Mickey Lemay had his case thrown out of court Friday morning. The senator's funeral was Friday afternoon.

It was an incredible jumble of events. The primary election broke upon us Saturday like a thunderclap upon the unsuspecting. The voters streamed to the polls dazed and weary. We in the newsroom were whipped senseless from trying to keep up with it all.

Darlene led in the returns, but the forty-four percent she polled was short of the absolute majority a candidate needed to be unopposed in the general election. She was forced into a runoff with the second-place finisher — Sheriff Lemay naturally — who checked in with thirty-seven percent of the vote. It was a respectable showing, but Lemay had learned his lesson and did no more dancing.

Darlene finished him off a month later in the runoff and guaranteed herself a seat in the Senate.

Just as the Mason County voters were turning their attention from politics to Thanksgiving, Senator-elect Darlene Christmas and Sheriff-elect Billy Emory, the newest family retainer, held a joint press conference. They accused Mickey Lemay of pocketing fines and fees and doctoring the books during his tenure as sheriff. They called for a probe by the State Bureau of Investigation.

Before the SBI agents could move in, Mickey Lemay slipped out of the state and was never heard from again.

Roger Christmas went back to Vanderbilt.

On assignment from Mr. Calhoun, Ellis Witby wrote a heart-warming story about how Darlene came to be the youngest senator ever elected in state history and how amply prepared she was for her new role.

The *Crier* won a national award for its aggressive reporting on Senator Christmas's death and the subsequent events. A week later I took a telephone call from the editor of the Capital *Times,* congratulating me on the award and offering me a job at his newspaper. The editor said he could use me to cover Capital County government and politics, and if I did a good job, I could expect to cover the legislature in a few years. The pay was twice what I was making at the *Crier.*

My parents were frail and failing, and their pensions were small. I needed the money and it was a dream job. I accepted.

I figured I was putting Mason County behind me forever, but I should have known better. Mason County clings to its own like a curse, as I would come to know only too well.

CHAPTER NINE

When I returned to the state capital, it was as though I was seeing it through two sets of eyes.

I remembered how I had felt when I arrived as a novitiate freshman, making her first solo foray into the world outside of Mason County. I had no personal identity then, only a sense that I would spend a time, an apprenticeship really, learning enough of life to return to the *Crier* as a full-fledged member of the newsroom.

The capital looked like a city in a dream, beset by tiny distortions that jarred my memory. There was a stationery store where a drugstore had been, the awnings on The General had gone from light green to dark, and didn't a diagonal path between two of the State University dormitories cut the opposite way?

I took a room in town at a place that usually rented to graduate students. Grateful for the price if not the quality of the accommodations, I figured I'd be working most of the time anyway.

The editor at the Capital *Times* was Anthony Allen Anderson III, and he appeared to be only a little older than I.

"Call me Trip," he said, jutting out a hand that was ink-stained in all the right places. A working editor.

"Trip, okay. Does that stand for 'Triple A' or 'the Third?' "

"Some say one thing, some the other. It's sort of a double-triple."

He laughed, so I did too. I liked him immediately. I had never, ever laughed with Mr. Calhoun.

"That sure was a good story you did when old Senator Christmas died," Trip said. "I know Darlene Christmas. I was a few years ahead of her, when I was at Harvard and she was at Radcliffe. I knew she'd get into politics, even if she had to do it on her old man's coffin. Well, I suppose I'll have to take her to lunch when the legislative session starts. Want to come along?"

"Only if I can bring a food taster," I said, and we laughed again.

Trip explained he was raised in Capital County, went off to Harvard and then returned to begin his climb through the ranks at the *Times,* which had been in his family for generations. The publisher was his father, Anthony Allen Anderson, Jr., known as "Andy." Substitute *newspaper* for *politics,* and Trip's life reminded me very much of Darlene Christmas's.

The county beat was better than I had dared hope for. The county commissioners were constantly at odds with the state government and the state university, both of which kept demanding additional services at no cost while acquiring property that automatically became tax exempt. The commissioners were probably the only men in the state who wouldn't stand up if the governor walked in or who didn't give a hoot about the university football team.

They were a crotchety, inbred set, unified in their resentment. There were five of them, and they met Monday afternoon and all day Tuesday, when it was inconvenient for any hard-working, tax-paying county voter to attend. The youngest had left sixty behind some time ago.

The senior member among them was one Colonel Rutherford Beamis Boggs, a veteran of some war in the distant past. He was brought to the meetings in a wheelchair by a trim little nurse in starched whites who made my heart go pitter-patter. Sometimes when the meetings got particularly cantankerous, she shared a smile with me. I needed all my concentration to keep taking notes.

Rarely did a session go by that Colonel Boggs didn't claim to be living in "the last occupied county in the South." He called the governor and the legislators "a bunch of carpetbaggers" and grumbled that the university's expansions "made it more carnivorous than a herd of dinosaurs." He probably knew from experience.

The job was fun, but I was lonely. There was nothing to stop me from watching some of the women's college teams play, as I had before, but I seemed to have passed some great divide and the athletes were a little young for me this time around. I admired the form, but not the substance.

Relief came one Saturday afternoon as I pushed a shopping cart through the fruit-and-vegetable aisle of the Piggledy Wiggledy grocery store. There, picking through the grapefruit display, was the little nurse who attended Colonel Boggs. She was dressed in her starched whites as she stood on tip-toe, reaching for a grapefruit in the back.

My mind was going places it should not have, as I watched her small hands squeezing and testing and looking for the perfect one.

"Hello," I said, because I couldn't think of anything else. It was humiliating for someone who made her living with words.

"Hello," she replied with a smile.

"I'm Jess Marceau. I see you at the commissioners' meetings."

"I know who you are. I read your articles in the paper. You're a very good writer."

"Thank you." I was becoming aware of a lot of tender places.

"My name is Sue Hill."

"You'll have to change it. That's much too complicated for me to remember."

She laughed. We were staring into each other's eyes. Hers were gentle and kind, and I knew mine were pleading.

She looked away first and glanced at my shopping

cart, which was filled mostly with some pretty awful frozen pot pies.

"Is that what you eat?" she said.

"I'm afraid it is. I'm a very bad cook."

"I'll be off duty at seven. Would you like supper?"

"I'd love it."

It turned out to be that Sue Hill shared an apartment with two other nurses, so we agreed to meet at my place. I went home and cleaned in a frenzy, and then sat in a chair and trembled while I waited for her. I was too nervous to do anything else.

She arrived at around seven-thirty, toting a bag of food. She was still in her nurse's uniform, her rubber-soled shoes going swish-swish-swish on the carpet.

"I raided the Colonel's pantry for us," she said. "He's got a cook named Lucy who can make a meal that will bring tears to your eyes. It's one of the benefits of working there."

She brought out some cold ham and fresh rolls, put potatoes on to boil and made a salad. I set the table.

I couldn't take my eyes off her. Suddenly I knew why women were always falling for someone in uniform. That nurse's outfit with its pressed seams and tailored lines was driving me wild, so white and crisp and resolutely virgin.

Our eyes were flirting as we ate and made small talk.

"So what war did Colonel Boggs fight in?" I asked.

"I'm not sure. I suppose it was the First World War or the Spanish American War, but it could have been the War of Eighteen Twelve, for all I know," she said.

She giggled, and I couldn't stop myself. I laid my hand on top of hers and held my breath. It was do or die.

She looked grave for a moment as she considered the situation. Then she said, "I have thought about this sometimes when the commission meetings run long."

She touched my cheek, and I quivered with the exquisite tension that comes in the moment before a first kiss. It had been a long time.

Our lips met and melted together, and I felt I could be on fire forever.

After a time I realized the table was separating us awkwardly, so I led her to my saggy couch, where we sank rapturously amid the lumpy cushions.

There is nothing in God's sweet universe like making love to a nurse. Sue Hill's touch was generous and caring, and there was no secret of the human body she could not find and unlock.

She stroked the back of my neck while her lips enflamed me, kissing me on my cheeks and mouth and in the little hollow where my shirt was open and inviting.

I slid my hands along the sides of her uniform, feeling its roughness, craving the softness I knew was underneath. I undid the buttons, and the smartness of the uniform caved slowly to reveal the tender curves of her breasts, so full on such a small woman.

"Oh, Lord," I groaned as I peeled the uniform away, "now I know why angels wear white."

"Why is that?"

"They're envious of the nurses here on earth."

"Because of this?" She lowered her body against mine, her skin as electric as silk. Her hands went everywhere, and like a good angel, she didn't stop until the second coming.

I despaired of returning the pleasure she had given me, but she whispered her desires and I obliged eagerly.

Every woman I have known since has benefited from the gentle mysteries of Sue Hill.

The next few months were the most perfect of my life. I wanted to make love with Sue and work for the Capital *Times* forever and never want for anything again. In a more enlightened age, I would have asked her to marry me.

It was not to be. Six months after I moved to Capital County, Trip called me into his office and said the newspaper was experiencing some financial difficulties.

"I'm sorry, Jess, but I'm going to have to let you go."

It was the last thing I expected. Sue and I cried a lot and talked about going off where we both could find work, but deep in our hearts we feared it was over for us.

I had just paid a month's rent and had another month put by, but that was it. I had eight weeks to find a new job. I didn't want to leave Capital County, but I didn't want to be unemployed either. I swallowed hard and telephoned Mr. Calhoun at the *Crier*.

He took my call, but he was remote. He didn't

have a job for me, he said, and didn't expect to. He wouldn't even consider me for freelance assignments. Something was very wrong, and it was clear I would never work at the *Crier* again.

I wrote letters to every newspaper within fifty miles of the capital and got turned down by each one. I wrote to every paper within a hundred miles, and it was the same thing.

By the end of the seventh week, I was getting desperate. I hadn't sent my folks a dime since I lost my job, and even though they didn't say anything, I knew they were feeling the pinch. Thank heavens Sue was bringing me the leavings of Colonel Boggs' larder, or who knows what I would have eaten.

Sharply at eight o'clock on Thursday morning of Week Seven, my telephone rang and a woman said, "Jess Marceau? Hold for Senator Christmas, please."

Darlene came on the line. "Jess," she said, "I heard you were out of work. I'm expanding my staff, and I need a press secretary. If you're interested, you may come in for an interview tomorrow morning at eight."

For a moment my vision blurred, disordered by some cosmic shift. I hesitated — teetered, really — and then took the only path I could.

"I'll be there," I said.

CHAPTER TEN

Darlene Christmas had a small office strategically located in the Statehouse, perfect to show she was a junior member of the Senate but definitely on the rise. It was situated just down the hall from the Senate leadership, which more than made up for its modest size.

Still, it was larger than the offices of the state representatives and positively spacious when compared to the quarters of the half-dozen or so Republicans who scandalized the state by getting themselves elected to the legislature. All of the Republicans, even the Senate minority leader, had offices in the basement. Perhaps it was impossible to keep the Republicans out of mind, but they certainly could be kept out of sight.

Darlene's father had served on the Senate Public Works Committee so he could tend to the folks back home by doling out a generous share of roadwork and other construction projects. The contractors loved him for it, the real estate agents did too, and so did the county commissioners and the bankers and the bond counselors and the laborers who toiled at scale.

Darlene, however, had a committee assignment that positioned her to be something more than a junior senator from Mason County. She sat on the Senate Finance Committee, a vastly powerful panel that drafted the state budget in conjunction with the House Appropriations Committee.

Nothing happened in state government without approval from the money committees. The seat was a plum for any senator and unheard-of for a newly elected member, but the governor himself had taken an interest in Darlene's career and urged the Senate leadership to assign her there.

Already there were whispers in the ornate Statehouse halls that Darlene could play politics with the best. Someday, it was said, she might run for lieutenant governor or attorney general, woman or not. The blood would tell.

I walked into Darlene's office while the secretaries were still getting their first cups of coffee. A receptionist smiled at me and buzzed the news of my arrival to the inner sanctum. A door was opened almost immediately, and Quinton Coombs ushered me past a scheduler into Darlene's office.

I was immediately disoriented. I did not see a classmate there, but the embodiment of the late Senator Christmas. I had never noticed before how much Darlene resembled her father, but here in this quiet Senate office with the somber curtains and overlarge desk, I saw him reflected in her nose and her cheekbones and the way she offered me her hand.

I found myself saying, really quite earnestly, "Senator, you don't know how much I appreciated your call."

"And you don't know how lucky I felt when I found out you might be available," Darlene said, giving me a smile of indescribable Southern charm. "Mr. Coombs, didn't I say when we decided to hire a press secretary, I hoped we could find someone like Jess Marceau?"

"That you did, Senator."

"We never dreamed, Jess, it might actually be you," Darlene said.

She spoke as though I was already working for her. I had brought along writing samples, but she never looked at them. She didn't ask me about my work at the Mason County *Crier*. She never inquired why I had been laid off from the Capital *Times*. She did ask what my salary had been.

"Oh, Jess, we've got to double that. I know your parents must be depending on you. By the way, how are they? Your momma was always so helpful to me at the library."

I stammered my answer and my thanks, and I began to feel very, very guilty for all the unkind thoughts I had harbored about the Christmases. Roger had been good to me. Darlene was being good to me. Finally I was seeing why so many people had counted on the Christmases for so many generations. I vowed to myself right then and there I would never let Darlene down, no matter what.

"When can you start?" she asked.

"Immediately. I'm ready to go to work now."

"Wonderful! Mr. Coombs, let's get all the paperwork out of the way, and we'll have a good old talk about what we need to do."

Quinton Coombs produced a raft of papers. "This one puts you on the Senate payroll. This one puts you on the campaign payroll when the Senate isn't in session. This one grants you access to the Capitol at all hours, and this one does the same for the County Courthouse back home. This one" — Coombs hesitated and glanced at it — "puts your signature on file at the Mason County Commercial Trust in case we have an emergency need for funds and we're here and you're there. This one does the same at this end."

I signed away, and then they took me to The General for a late breakfast. Darlene seemed triumphant. Quinton Coombs looked smug. I felt flattered and very, very relieved.

When I called my folks that evening and told them about my new job, they were so happy they cried.

Little did I know, but the trap had been set.

Everything seemed fine. I fit easily into the staff, slipping into the practice of referring to Darlene as "Senator," the way nurses speak of their doctors.

"Senator needs you," a staff member would say,

or "Who has the copies of Senator's speech?" or to the public, "Do you have an appointment with Senator?"

Sometimes Senator worked in the capital, and that was bliss, because I went home at night to Sue. We ate dinners by candlelight, made love, traded stories about Senator Christmas and Colonel Boggs, and remained philosophical about the telephone calls bringing word of emergencies — political or medical — that not infrequently summoned one or the other of us for extra duty in the evening.

Sometimes Senator worked back in Mason County, and that was tolerable, because soon I would be going home to Sue.

The work wasn't particularly hard. I wrote speeches for important appearances (Senator had a talent for off-the-cuff remarks at more informal events), set up press interviews and helped to answer the voluminous constituent mail. Quinton Coombs, with his long history with the family, was Senator's official spokesman, not I.

Although the staff jumped to Senator's courteous orders, our pace was otherwise fairly relaxed. It wasn't an election year, and Senator didn't undertake many legislative initiatives, preferring to curry favor with the leadership by working on theirs and biding her time. With a seat as safe as hers, she had plenty of it to burn.

The end came about a year into my employment. It was a sleepy afternoon, after we'd been to a meeting of the Mason City Rotary Club. I was answering a constituent letter when the receptionist interrupted me.

"Senator wants to see you in her office," she said.

It was not unusual. I went in. Waiting there with Senator were two grim-looking men with haircuts so short they could only have been law enforcement officers. Senator said icily, "Jess, these gentlemen are with the State Bureau of Investigation. They have some questions to ask you."

My heart started beating fast, although I didn't know why. The trap was sprung.

The SBI agents accused me of siphoning money from Senator's campaign treasury. It had started small, with checks of $25 made out to petty cash, until it reached a series of withdrawals of $250 for phony expenses and reimbursements, thousands of dollars in all. The money was stashed in an account under a fictitious name, with me as a cosigner, in a bank I had never heard of.

"This can't be," I said, a nightmare sweat upon me.

Then in a flash I figured it out. I remembered the papers I had signed when I went to work for Senator. It was a setup. It was why Senator had hired me. It was a payback for writing the story about her father.

I looked at her. She knew I knew, and she calmly and coldly nodded.

"Oh, my God," Mamie said. It was very late, and we were in our favorite place, on the porch glider with my head on her lap.

"Yes. I had been framed perfectly. I had no defense. My signature was on everything. The SBI agents dialed up Sheriff Emory, and they took me right to the basement of the courthouse and put me in a cell. It was bizarre — direct from Senator's office to jail, all in the same building," I said. "I was crazed. I couldn't even phone Sue. She found out the way everybody else did — by reading it in the newspapers. It was weeks until I talked to her again, after I was sent away to the state prison in Red Oak. I told her what happened, and even though she believed me, I told her I didn't want to see her again. I couldn't bear the humiliation. That was the last I saw her."

I was surprised how much it still hurt.

"I couldn't get a lawyer to defend me, and the court finally appointed Josh Tomlinson. I spent most of my time arguing with him because he wanted me to plead guilty and take a plea bargain. The more I insisted I was innocent, the madder he got. He was the most reluctant lawyer I ever saw."

"I know. I went to the trial. Josh was a disgrace to the profession," Mamie said.

"The trial was a joke. Senator sat there like the woman scorned. The *Crier* wrote reams of stories about 'Senator betrayed.' "

"I remember," Mamie said.

"I don't think my own parents believed I was innocent. If the jurors hadn't stalled long enough to get a free lunch, I'd have been convicted in minutes. I did six months at Red Oak. While I was in jail, my folks died seventeen days apart. It's said you can't die of a crushed heart, but I think they did. They gave up from the mortification. When I got out, I just drifted. I didn't want to see anyone I had ever known, didn't want to have any explaining to do. To tell you the truth, I don't have much recollection of those years away. Then one day I just sort of woke up and decided enough was enough. I had to go back. And then I found you."

Mamie stroked my hair for a while. Then she said, "Let me tell you what you don't know."

"What is it?"

"It's about me. They wanted me to prosecute you. I don't know why, probably some kind of loyalty test since we'd been friends.

"I refused. I knew you. I knew you couldn't have done it, no matter how high they piled up the evidence. When I heard you say in court you were innocent, I knew I was right."

"I can't tell you what it means to hear that, even after all this time."

"The county attorney was furious with me. About two weeks after your trial, one of the sheriff's dogs sniffed marijuana in my car when it was parked outside the courthouse. It had been planted, of course, but like you I didn't have much of a defense." Mamie looked grim. The resentment hadn't left her yet. "They wanted me out, but they didn't want another spectacle like the one you put them through, so I was able to go quietly. I resigned from the county attorney's office, accepted disbarment and agreed to leave Mason County, in exchange for not being prosecuted. I knew they would try me if they had to, and I would lose. It seemed better this way. I left Mason County, but not by much. I've been here ever since, living in this house, running that tacky little restaurant and waiting, I expect, for the South to rise again or you to return and clear your name, whichever came first."

"You should have bet on the South," I said.

"Maybe. Maybe not."

"All of what's happened to you, it's my fault."

"Hush, Jess. Lawyers call that kind of talk 'blaming the victim.' It's wrong."

"I shouldn't have come back. Who knows what will happen now?"

CHAPTER ELEVEN

In the morning I told Mamie I didn't want to go to the restaurant with her. I wanted time to think. She looked dubious but she didn't fight me. I suppose she realized we were in too deep for me to run.

I poured the last of the coffee into my cup and wandered out to the porch, which had become my favorite place. I sat on the glider and listened to the birds and the faraway bark of a nervous dog, and I pondered.

I pondered that Senator Christmas ought not to

get away with what she had done to us. I pondered about how powerful she was. I pondered that as low as I had fallen, Senator Christmas probably had ways to make me fall farther and I could be taking Mamie with me when I went. I pondered about how I had to do something, anyway, or at least try. It was not a happy ponder.

When Mamie came home, I said, "Whatever happened to Roger Christmas?"

"He's been gone a long while, almost as long as you. He poked his way through Vanderbilt, then dallied through law school and came home. He went to work in the Senate office, although nobody thought he wanted to. It was generally believed he was only staying around because their mother wanted him to, and sure enough, after she died, he packed up and went away. The last I heard, he was practicing law in Davenport."

"I've been through there," I said. "It's kind of a seedy little town for a county seat."

"Well, you know what they say about Middle County. It's smack in the middle of nothing."

"I think I'd like to pay a call on Roger Christmas."

"Are you sure that's such a good idea?"

"I've been thinking, Mamie. He's the one that got all this started. Maybe he's gentleman enough to get it ended."

"But, Jess, he's still a Christmas."

"A reluctant Christmas, remember?"

"How reluctant? He's had plenty of time to put this right and he hasn't lifted a finger. What makes you think he'll do something now?"

I had to concede the point. "Well, what else is there?" When she didn't say a word, I said, "If it's all right with you, I'd like to borrow the car tomorrow."

In the morning I put on my old, fraying clothes. There was no sense in letting Roger think I had amounted to anything.

I dropped Mamie off at the restaurant and drove eighty miles west to Davenport, as feeble an excuse for a county seat as ever there was one. The timber lords had cleared out the countryside long ago and left it to the scavengers. It was the dregs of the state, and the last place anyone would look for a Christmas.

I parked the little Ford in front of the courthouse and walked into a drugstore across the street, searching for a phone booth and telephone book. Roger was listed, all right. As a matter of fact, he couldn't have been any closer. His office was a second-floor walkup above the drugstore.

Outside, now that I knew what I was looking for, I found a dusty entryway and a fading sign: *Roger Christmas, Attorney at Law.* If you didn't know it was there, you'd never find it.

I climbed the stairs, not nearly as nervous as I thought I'd be, and found him inside a one-room chamber — no anteroom, no secretary, no associate, just Roger in an office cluttered with law books and files, empty paper coffee cups and old sandwich wrappers. There were graduate students who would have scorned this setup.

Roger needed a haircut. His white shirt had been washed so many times it was graying. His tie was pulled away from his throat, his vest was unbuttoned and his jacket was tossed indifferently over an easy chair. Although it was early, he looked as though he had been up for hours. There wasn't a laugh line in his face.

When he saw who it was, his shoulders drooped and he exhaled, like a soul expiring. I expect he wished he was.

"Well, well," Roger said.

He didn't move his jacket or ask me to sit down, so I stood in the doorway, just as polite as my mother had taught me. Roger was still a Christmas, and I still wasn't.

"Are you busy?" I asked.

"Busy? In Davenport?"

"It's a manner of speaking."

"I see."

"Roger, what are you doing here?"

"What am I doing here? I'm practicing law. A little real estate, some wills, the occasional bankruptcy or whatever, enough to stay occupied. It turns out my sainted father was correct to insist I acquire a profession."

"That's not what I meant."

"I expect not. But that's the point, Jess. I'm here to try to forget what I'm doing here."

We looked frankly at each other, telegraphing memories and pain. At that moment we may have been the two unhappiest people in the world — certainly in Middle County.

"Roger, I need your help."

"No, you don't. You need to leave here and keep going and never come back. You haven't made it home yet, have you?"

"I'm afraid I have. I came from there."

He winced. "That was a mistake, a big, big mistake. You don't ever want to be where my sister can find you."

"I don't want to run anymore. I didn't do anything wrong, Roger. All I did was write a story. Don't you feel anything for me?"

"I gave a story to a reporter. That's all."

"That wasn't all. You let a friend go down."

"I can't blame you for thinking that."

"It wasn't just the story, Roger. You could have warned me not to take that press secretary's job."

"As if it would have mattered."

"It would have. I would have listened to you."

Roger looked very agitated. He stood up. "You don't understand. *It would not have mattered.* It wouldn't have mattered, because Darlene was ready to track you to the ends of the earth."

"But she —"

"Listen to me, Jess. *Listen to me.* You still don't understand what she can do.

"Do you think it was luck that brought you to that job at the Capital *Times?* Hell, no. Darlene made it happen. Trip Anderson is an old friend of hers. They've known each other since Harvard. They used to double date, because Trip was going out with the sister of a guy that Darlene was seeing. You didn't know that, did you? Trip only hired you to fire you. Then he and Mrs. Letard at the *Crier* made sure you were blacklisted at every other paper in the state, because that's what Darlene wanted. She arranged it so you didn't have any choice other than to become her press secretary. That's what she can do."

I couldn't believe what I was hearing. Roger wasn't finished, though.

"Suppose I had warned you off. Suppose you'd found work as a librarian or an accountant or a waitress. She would have found a way to get you fired or framed — whatever it took to remind Mason County that no one meddles with the Christmases and gets away with it, not ever." Roger paused as though he was wrapping up his closing argument for a jury. "Look what she did to Sheriff Lemay. Look what she did to your friend Mamie. My sister can do whatever she wants to do, and I sure as hellfire can't stop her."

This was monstrous, worse than I had imagined. "Roger, you mean all those things I thought were coincidences, you mean she *planned* them?"

"There are no coincidences in Mason County."

"Oh, my God."

"That's why I can't help you, Jess. There's nothing I can do."

"Roger, you're my last hope."

"Sorry. What you need to do is get out of here. Get out of this state. Go to California, go North, go anywhere. Just go."

"You're her brother. There must be something you know, something you can do. How can you live with yourself without trying? You have to stand up to her."

"You've forgotten. I'm the black sheep of the family. A black sheep doesn't have to do anything. Don't waste any more of your time."

I got to Mamie's restaurant a little before closing and let myself in through the back. Mamie was sitting at her table with an official-looking letter in her hand, and I could tell from her expression it wasn't good news.

Great. All I could do was add to it.

"Uh-oh," I said. "You want to go first, or shall I?"

"Mine's quicker."

"All right."

"This is a letter from the State Bureau of Revenue. They're going to audit the restaurant."

It wasn't hard to guess who was behind it. "She sits on the Senate Finance Committee. That gives her jurisdiction over the Bureau of Revenue," I said.

"Apparently."

"So she can reach across the county line, too. Mamie, this is my fault. I am so sorry."

"It's not your fault. Stop saying that. Anyway, my books are in order and I pay my taxes. There's nothing for them to find."

We avoided each other's eyes. Just because there was nothing to find, it didn't mean the auditors would come up empty. We both were living proof of that.

CHAPTER TWELVE

The audit was two weeks away. Mamie spent hours and hours going over her records, and she even pulled out some of her old tax law books.

"I'm prepared for this the way I used to get ready for trials," she said. "I'm scared, but I'm sort of enjoying it. Isn't that crazy?"

I wasn't enjoying it at all. Some days I smoldered. Some days I despaired. Mamie bore my moods affectionately. When she worked on her records in the evening, she lugged everything out to the porch so I could laze next to her and let my bad tempers drain away, consoled by her presence. She never concentrated so hard that she couldn't find time to ruffle my hair.

Mamie was leaving nothing to chance. She put those records through an inspection that would have made a marine drill sergeant proud. Then she rang up Pete Lebeau, an accountant who had gone to school with us, and asked him whether he would take a look.

Pete was obliging. His office was on the main drag in Mason City, and Mamie asked me to run the records in.

It was Friday morning. The audit was scheduled for Monday. I drove Mamie's car into town and carted her records to Pete. He told me to stop back before lunch and he'd be done with them.

It was silly to drive back to Stone Bridge and turn right around, so I had some time to kill. I decided to stay in town, maybe read a magazine at the library or get a cup of coffee at the drugstore. I should have known better. Mason City was no place for me.

As I neared the courthouse, Sheriff Emory came outside and gave me the look a man gives a squirrel when he has a rifle in his hands.

"How you doing, Jess?" he said.

"Fine, Sheriff, thank you kindly," I said before my voice strangled in my throat.

"Is that your car you drove in?"

"No, sir. It's —"

"Do you have a driver's license?"

"Yes, sir, I do." I lifted my license out of my wallet and cursed my fingers for trembling.

He glanced at it and asked, "Is that your right address?"

"No, sir. I've just arrived in Stone Bridge and —"

"Do you have a paying job?"

"Not exactly. I'm —"

"When you got to Stone Bridge, did you register with the sheriff? Convicted felons are supposed to do that."

"I'm sorry, I didn't. But as soon as I leave here, I'll —"

"No address, no job, no registration. Jess, I've got to take you in for vagrancy."

"Sheriff, in the name of —"

"Do you want to come quietly, or do you want me to get out the handcuffs?"

I went quietly, although there was a scream inside me that could have blown the gates off Kingdom Come. Sheriff Emory took my arm and guided me down the steps to the courthouse basement, down to the shadows that lingered there, down to the same small cell that waited as patiently as a spider for my return.

I think I was out of my head in there. My mind raced from image to image like a movie camera out of control. I saw the judge sentencing me. I saw the prison dining hall at Red Oak with the long line of sullen women waiting for what passed for a meal and wearing drab uniforms that were never laundered well enough. I saw Senator saying, "Jess, these gentlemen are with the State Bureau of Investigation. They have some questions to ask you."

I lay flat on the low, dark bench in the cell and let the nightmares and hallucinations do their work.

They were what I had fled from, and now they were back.

I don't know how long I lay there in that chamber of shadows and unmeasured time, but by and by I heard footsteps, followed by some of the sweetest words I ever heard.

"Come on. You're being let out," a deputy sheriff said.

He took me to the sheriff's office, where Mamie waited, grim and seething. I was astonished at seeing her but had enough sense to say nothing, for fear of revealing my ragged condition. Sheriff Emory was nowhere in sight.

Mamie took me to the car. I eased into the passenger's seat and collapsed. The sweat ran into my eyes faster than I could wipe it away.

"How did you find me?" I asked.

"Pete got concerned when you didn't return on time and phoned me. I had sense enough to call an old friend in the county attorney's office and found out the courthouse was humming like a beehive over your arrest. My friend — never mind who — was kind enough to drive out for me and bring me back. Then the sheriff and I had a little talk about the law, and we agreed that he would let you out and you wouldn't press charges against him."

"As though I'd have the nerve for it."

"Well, he didn't know that for sure."

"Mamie, it was just as though Sheriff Emory was lying in wait for me. He had a trap all set so he could put me in jail. He wouldn't have done that unless he was told to."

"That's what I think, too."

"An audit for you. Jail for me. Roger Christmas was right. She can do whatever she wants. We can't fight her."

"Jess, we're in too far to back away now."

"If I go back to prison, I'll go mad."

Mamie didn't answer. Instead, she drove us to Pete Lebeau's office and told me to wait in the car while she retrieved her books.

I sat there. It took all the will I had left not to whimper.

The next day was Saturday, and I was too despondent to go into the restaurant with Mamie. I took one of those long walks the way I used to, not seeing anything, not knowing where I'd been, just blindly tramping and tramping and tramping until I found myself back where I started.

I didn't want to go with her on Sunday either, but she said I had to and we had our first fight.

"Jess, you can't just sit here."

"The hell I can't."

"Listen, the audit is tomorrow, and I have to get ready for it. I need you to help in the kitchen. I want us to stay late and do a little extra cleaning too. You never know, but Senator might send in the Board of Health next."

I sulked, but I went. The first hours were a blur, but eventually I roused myself and started feeling bad about the way I was treating Mamie. By the time she closed for the evening I was ready to make it up to her, and I cleaned with a purpose.

We were in the kitchen. Mamie was writing up the list of supplies she needed for the next week, and I was scrubbing the sink. I got to thinking that this was the way we began, and I glanced over my shoulder at Mamie.

She was looking at me. Actually, it was more than looking. It was lusting, her dark eyes tracing the curve of my hip as I bent over the sink.

When she saw she'd been caught, she laughed and said playfully, "Want a beer? Owner's private stock."

I knew those words. Clearly we were thinking the same thing. "Sure," I said.

She fetched two bottles and I joined her at the table. She drank a little and then leaned over and kissed me, the beer still on her lips. It was a tender, insistent kiss, and I who had come to dread flashbacks found myself having one that could make me want to dwell in the past forever.

"The criminal always returns to the scene of the crime," I murmured when Mamie finally let me up for air.

"I think we could do with a reenactment," she said.

She shucked her shirt off with the eagerness of a child headed for a swimming hole, and I cupped my hands around her breasts and felt the heat rising from them.

We kissed again, and I slipped her shorts and panties from her waist and slid them admiringly down her smooth, rounded thighs. She started to unbutton my shirt, but I couldn't wait. I pulled her to the floor with my clothes still on, kissing her, running my hands urgently over her body, searching her, tantalizing her.

She twisted away and pawed at my clothes. "Let's get these off," she said, and we tugged them away.

The kitchen tiles felt cool beneath me, and I rolled onto my back and pulled Mamie on top to feel the warmth of her body against mine. It was like standing in front of a blast furnace on a winter day, with your senses tingling like mad from the dueling sensations.

I wanted Mamie bad. She started nipping at me with her mouth and teasing me with her fingers, and then she had to smother me with a kiss because my breathing was getting louder and louder and we *were* in a commercial zone, even if it was a Sunday night.

"Wow," I said wonderingly and lay limp.

Mamie took my unresisting hands and made them stroke her cheeks and her breasts and her hips and then guided them between her squirming thighs.

Playfully I pretended to pull my hands away, but she clasped them there between her legs, and I found just enough give in the pressure for the gentle touch she loved. In a moment she was rocking hard and moaning from deep in her throat.

"Quick-Draw McGraw, that's me," she said.

"And not a pot pie in sight."

Slowly we collected ourselves. We were nearly ready to go when Mamie said, "Just a minute. I want to change the tape in the cash register before we leave."

We walked out front. Behind the big picture window, where the shade was pulled down, we saw a shadowy figure silhouetted by the street lights. It was lurking jerkily and menacingly, as though it could barely contain the violence within.

We pulled up in a dead stop, the sweat of our

passion turning chill. Mamie recovered first and she whispered, "I've got a gun in the back, and I'm going to get it."

I stood alone and watched the figure's slow, lurching pace as it closed on us, then retreated, then closed in its relentless, dark dance.

Mamie returned. "I'm going to stand back here," she whispered. "You go fling open the door, and maybe we can scare him off."

I would have liked to suggest that *I* stay back and *she* go to the door, but I couldn't. Being a convicted felon, I wasn't allowed to touch the gun. I had to be the one to go.

This was no time for panic. I forced myself to keep breathing, and I crept to the door, unlocked it quietly and then let it fly.

Startled, the figure leaped back, and I got a good look at him.

"Roger Christmas! What are you doing here?"

Roger smiled. "I hope I'm doing good," he said.

CHAPTER THIRTEEN

"Roger Christmas, you about scared us to death," Mamie said.

"I'm sorry," Roger said gallantly. He laughed self-consciously. "I've about scared myself to death. I can't imagine what's given me the gumption to come here. I'd much rather be hiding out in Davenport."

"Come in the back," Mamie said. "I'll put on a pot of coffee."

We went into the kitchen. I glanced around quickly, afraid there might be some clue left from our unbridled romancing to give us away, but the only hint was the warm blush I could feel on my face, and Roger didn't seem to notice.

Roger's appearance surprised me. He was wearing khaki slacks and a white sports shirt, both neatly pressed. He'd gotten a haircut and was recently shaved. He looked better at leisure than he had at his office, and he had that choirboy look of a drunk who discovered sobriety and really meant to stay clean.

"I thought you were done with me for good," I said.

"I thought I was, too. But you said something to me, and you were right. How could I go on living with myself if I didn't at least try to stand up to my sister? So here I am."

Hope tried to rise within me, but I kicked its legs out from under it before it could get too far. There had been too many setbacks over too many years. Hope was going to have to wait until I was sure it could stand up good and sturdy.

We sat at the table. The only sound was the raspy gurgle of the coffee perking, as we waited for Roger to collect his thoughts.

"There was something else you said, Jess. You said I had to know something that could stop my sister, and there is. I'll tell you about it, but you can't tell who told you, and you have to leave me out of whatever you do. Promise?"

It was a pretty big promise. The last time I struck a deal like that with Roger Christmas, I went to prison. Still, what other choice did we have?

I looked at Mamie. Mamie looked at me. Seeing no objection, as the lawyers say, we nodded our acceptance. It was so solemn the only thing missing was a blood oath.

"Is the coffee ready?" Roger asked.

Mamie poured. Roger fiddled with the cream and sugar, taste-testing his coffee twice before he got it right. I was sloshing mine down, black as usual, to keep myself occupied. Roger's dawdling was doing nothing for my nerves.

"There is something," Roger said. "It's been in my family for generations. I can remember my grandfather being involved, but it started long before him. Then my father took over, and now it's Darlene. Let me put it this way. Do you know what folks do Sunday nights in Mason County?"

Why won't he get on with this? I wondered tensely.

Mamie was more charitable. "Stay home with their Bibles, I expect," she said.

"No, ma'am. They're not even home with their TVs. They're at Quinton Coombs' farm, east of town, and do you know what they're doing?"

"I expect the Bibles aren't part of this, either," I said.

"They are cockfighting," Roger said.

Cockfighting. The royal diversion of Henry VIII. The passion of George Washington and Thomas Jefferson. Cockfighting had been driven underground generations ago, and yet it still flourished, its devotees drawn by the blood lust of a fight to the finish.

For years I had heard rumors of cockfights in Mason County, but I had never known for sure.

"On a typical Sunday night," Roger said, "if the

birds are the best, the betting can run into the thousands of dollars. I've seen it. My sister, like my father and grandfather before her, presides over every match. She gets a cut of every bet. She's the master of the show. Best of all, she can guarantee that the cockfights never get raided. No one gets arrested for gambling. No one gets their birds confiscated. They're safer cockfighting with Senator Christmas than they would be at home with their Bibles." He paused. "Unless you all want to do something about it."

Roger drained his coffee cup. He drummed his fingers on the table. He was flushed, just as you would expect of someone who had just sold out his own sister.

"What happens if we go to Sheriff Emory?" Mamie asked.

"He's a regular participant."

"I should've guessed. What about the State Bureau of Investigation?"

"She controls their budget from the Senate Finance Committee. They don't want any part of investigating her."

"The FBI?"

"I wouldn't trust any of the local agents."

"What about going to the *Crier*?"

"The publisher's son owns some of the best birds around."

Mamie considered. "You're not giving us much to work with," she said.

"It's the best I can do," Roger said. "Meanwhile, let me give you some advice. My sister can always use people like you — people she's turned into outcasts and don't have much left to lose. If you pretend to make your peace with her, she'll take you back, even give you work, and you'll be able to infiltrate the cockfighting. I know how she operates." He coughed self-consciously. "That's it. I've had my say. I'm going back to Davenport now, and I don't want to know how anything turns out."

Roger took his leave. His handshake was nerveless, his departure the hasty retreat of a man who knows where the county line is and makes it his business to be across it.

We sat, and the silence froze around us like a tomb in winter.

"Can we afford to trust him?" Mamie asked.

"Can we afford not to?" I answered.

About the twelfth time that night I heard Mamie flip her pillow, looking for a cool spot, I said, "You getting any sleep?"

"No. Are you?"

"Not hardly. Let's go out on the porch."

We took our pillows and shuffled out to the glider. I found myself watching the flying creatures of the night dive-bombing the screens. Mostly there were the pale fluttery moths, hitting with soft thumps, and an array of dark, hard-shelled insects striking in fury, whining like tiny buzz saws of Satan.

"I think I have a plan," Mamie said.

A half an hour later, I nodded. It was a good plan. We kicked it around a little longer, making refinements.

"We'll sleep on it," Mamie said. "If we don't come up with anything else by morning, why, we'll go ahead."

Eventually we drowsed, waking when the early rays of the sun steamed the air around us into a summery cauldron. We looked dismally at each other.

"Can you think of anything else?" Mamie asked.

"No. What about you?"

"No."

"Well then."

There was nothing to do but get on with it. We went inside and dressed for our parts. Mamie got spiffed up like a lawyer, the better to do battle. I put on the frayed clothes I wore when I arrived. If, as Roger said, Senator liked to collect outcasts, I might as well look like the ex-con I was.

We drove into Mason City and parked at the courthouse. It was early, and deliberately so, too early for Sheriff Emory to be poking around or for his deputies to be paying attention.

Mamie gathered her records and headed for the State Bureau of Revenue office for her audit. I kept walking until I came to an alcove near Senator Christmas's office, where I could loiter and listen undetected.

Soon I heard the dull tread of Quinton Coombs and the jangle of his keys as he arrived to unlock the office. No one — not even staff — was allowed in before he got there to oversee Senator's business.

He was followed shortly by the quick, excuse-me steps of Beverly Billingsley, the receptionist, who never came late but always acted as though she was afraid she had. Working for Quinton Coombs could have that effect.

I waited. After a time I heard the steady gait of Senator Christmas, and I realized in that moment that I hadn't seen her since the day she sat coolly in the back of the courtroom while the guards hustled me out the prisoners' door. Ellis Witby and the other reporters had swarmed to her like worker bees to their queen to ask whether she was satisfied with the verdict? I had twisted my head to try to catch her reply, but she said only three words: "No comment, boys."

I was sweating, and it wasn't the heat, but that was all right. There was no shame in being afraid of Senator. I was sure she'd take it as a compliment.

I stepped out and cleared my throat. "Senator, could I speak with you?"

"Why, Jess Marceau," she said, sounding my name like a sentence of death.

Quinton Coombs was instantly at her side. He was looking ugly, since I had managed to get to Senator without going through him, but she stopped him with a glance. Then she gave me one of those Southern belle smiles, all teeth and no eyes, and said, "Come inside."

We went into her private office, and I was relieved when she didn't invite Quinton Coombs along. Senator closed the door, put her purse in a closet and sat at her desk.

I wasn't just sweating now, I was shaking. Senator took one look at me and buzzed through on her intercom. "Miss Billingsley, would you be kind enough to bring Miss Marceau a glass of water, please?"

In a moment the receptionist entered and handed me a glass, which had the seal of the state Senate on it. I used to drink out of those all the time, when I had worked there. These repeated jerks back to the past weren't doing anything for my state of mind.

I drained the glass. The receptionist reclaimed it and departed. I guess she'd heard I was a thief and didn't want to leave anything lying around.

"Why have you come to see me?" Senator said.

"Because I want to come back. I am terribly, terribly sorry for the trouble I caused you. I was wrong, and I can't live with it anymore. If you'll let me, I want to come home."

Senator regarded me steadily. Through the years she had acquired the card-shark instincts of a politician who never falls for a sucker story.

"You've been staying across the line with Mamie Todd, haven't you?" Senator said.

"Yes, Senator. I've been helping in her restaurant. She feels the same way I do, and she would have come with me — except . . ."

"Except she's at the revenue office."

"Yes."

"Those revenue agents can always find something."

"I've heard that. We sure could use your help, Senator."

There. I had said the magic words. Either she took us back, or she could have me arrested for trying to influence a state official.

Senator touched her intercom button. "Miss Billingsley, could you ask Mr. Coombs to come in, please?"

He was there before the receptionist finished saying, "Of course, Senator." He must have been waiting at the door, his insides twisting over being shut out.

"Mr. Coombs, I need you to run down to the revenue office. Tell those boys I'm interested in Miss Todd's case."

"But, Senator —"

She silenced him with a look that could have started a forest fire.

"Yes, Senator," he said.

Sweat was trickling down my face. Senator gave me a friendly smile and said, "Can you use some work, Jess?"

"You bet, Senator. Anything."

"I've got some Cabinet secretaries coming to town this afternoon. I'm having them back to the house for an informal reception. I can always use another hand to help out. Are you interested?"

"Sure thing."

"You remember where the house is?"

I flashed back to the night I waited behind the bushes with Mr. Calhoun for the undertaker to come out. "Of course, Senator."

"All right. Be there at four. Ask for Len Buckworth. He'll show you what to do." She gave my clothes a critical glance. "He'll have a uniform for you. White shirt and slacks. I don't think we'll bother with jackets today. Wear white shoes if you have them."

"I do." I had them from my years of restaurant

work. "Thank you, Senator. I can't tell you how grateful I am."

"It's good to have you back, Jess. I've enjoyed our little talk."

She offered me her hand. Since there was no ring to kiss, I simply shook it and left.

CHAPTER FOURTEEN

I didn't wait at the car very long before Mamie skipped out of the courthouse and joined me.

"So you succeeded," she said as she drove us away.

"How do you know?"

"Elementary, my dear Watson," Mamie said. "There I was, getting grilled by these three auditors, who looked as though they smiled about as often as the faces on Mount Rushmore. They were really giving me the business, and I'm sorry to admit this, Jess, but my lawyer's juices were flowing and it was sort of fun, even though I knew they would find whatever they wanted to find. At least I wasn't making it easy for them. Then there was a knock at the door, and the lead auditor was called out. After a time he came for the other two and they left, and then they all piled back in. They asked me a few more routine questions and said they'd get back to me, and it was over." She giggled, very unlawyerlike. "It was like prepping for the bar exam and instead being asked to recite 'Three Blind Mice.' It could only have meant one thing. Senator got to them and told them to stop, and that had to be on account of you."

"Brilliant deduction, Sherlock. You did figure it out," I said.

"So what happened in there?" Mamie asked. After I told her, she said, "Well, that's the first step. We have some breathing room, at least."

"Yes. It's a little like being a treed cat. It's all right as long as we sit here, but sooner or later we've got to climb down."

We went back to the restaurant, where Honey Chiles and a part-time waitress had handled the breakfast crowd and were getting ready for lunch.

A few hours later I took the car and drove to the Christmas home. It was my first trip there since I had worked as Senator's press secretary, and she invited the staff out for an occasional barbecue. In those days, though, I entered through the front door. This time I went around back to the service entrance and presented myself to Len Buckworth, an old family retainer who had been in charge of the residence longer than Quinton Coombs had taken care of the Senate office.

He greeted me without a trace of suspicion, handed me a white uniform and gave me my assignment for the reception. All I had to do was empty the ashtrays and clear away the used glasses while the guests were there and then chip in for the general cleanup afterwards.

It was easy work. I blended in with the rest of the help with no trouble. I was careful not to make any eye contact with the guests and especially not with Senator.

She called me over when I was done and surprised me by handing me a check for a hundred dollars.

"I didn't do anything to deserve this kind of money!" I said.

"You will," she replied.

Mamie was smiling when I got home, until she got a whiff of me. "Phew! You smell like an ashtray."

"Occupational hazard. You want me to take a shower?"

"Never mind. Let's go out on the porch. There's a breeze. Maybe you'll air out. But it might be nice if you showered before bedtime," she said with a wink.

"You bet."

"How did it go at the house?"

"Fine. Easy work. But look at this check."

"Heavenly days. What was that for?"

"Hell if I know. I told Senator I didn't deserve it, and all she said was, 'You will.' "

"I don't much like the sound of that."

"Me either." I handed Mamie the check. "Listen, I

want you to have this. You've been taking care of everything."

"So what? You keep it. You're entitled to have money of your own."

"I don't have any desire for it." It was true. I had gone without for so many years that I no longer cared, and I certainly wasn't interested in developing any attachment to checks from Senator.

Mamie smiled at me indulgently. "All right. I'll keep it for you and be your money manager."

"That will be fine."

"Now that that's taken care of, are you ready to get on with our plan?" Mamie said, the prosecutor's look returning to her eyes.

"I expect so. Tell me about this guy again?"

"Norman. Norman Turkle. He was an FBI agent here when I was with the county attorney's office. Everybody called him Norman the Terrible. He was a nice man, but he hated crooks, and he didn't trust anyone in Mason County."

"Smart," I said.

"He did trust me, though. As luck would have it, he knew me before he got here through his son. I'd met Little Norm in law school. We were in the same study group, and every now and then Norman the Terrible would show up and take all of us poor law students to dinner. Of course, I called him Mr. Turkle in those days. The Turkles were Yankees, from up north in Ohio, but we all hit it off just fine. In fact, listening to Norman the Terrible talk about crooks was one of the things that made me want to be a prosecutor. As luck would have it, he was transferred here shortly after I started work at the county attorney's office. He used to warn me Mason

County was corrupt, although he didn't go into any details. He said I shouldn't get too close to the power structure here."

"I'd say you succeeded," I said drily.

"No comments from the peanut gallery, please. Anyway, Norman eventually got assigned to Washington, and I figured that would be the last I saw of him. Then he showed up in the restaurant about a year ago. Said he'd retired and moved back to Ohio, but his wife died and he didn't feel like staying where all the memories were, so he moved here. He said Mason County might be the most corrupt he'd ever seen, but it also had the best fishing. He'd gone to the courthouse to look me up and found out where I was, so he wanted to stop by. He told me if I ever needed a friend to give him a call." She sighed. "I'd say now is a time we need a friend, wouldn't you?"

I stayed on the porch while Mamie went to the kitchen phone to call Norman. She kept the conversation at the level of "Norman-this-is-Mamie-and-how-is-Little-Norm." With modern technology, you never knew who could be listening in. Still, the tone in her voice said something was up, and she easily wangled us an invitation for a visit.

Mamie came back to the porch. "We'll drive over directly after we close the restaurant tomorrow."

Even for Mason County, Norman the Terrible lived out in the boondocks. He had a little cottage along a branch of the Lazy River, where the fish were always jumping and the cattails grew high. A lonely, dusty road meandered to his place, and Mamie had to drive slowly so the headlights could pick up the dips and curves.

We spotted Norman's house long before we got there. It was the only light for miles. We were truly in the middle of nowhere. The stars blazed overhead in prehistoric splendor, and the trees rustled as though they had secrets to keep. It was so peaceful, so different from the turmoil inside me.

Norman answered Mamie's knock quickly and invited us in. He had one of those manly dwellings, with lots of knotty wood paneling and paintings of outdoorsy scenes. The aroma of coffee from his dinner still lingered.

"This is a treat. I don't get much company." Norman smiled so affectionately at Mamie that I liked him right away.

"Well, you don't have to be a stranger," Mamie said. "You can stop by the restaurant any time and even have a meal on the house. Now that you're not a lawman, you can take it without worrying that it's a bribe."

They laughed, and then Norman said, "To tell the truth, Mamie, I was a little afraid to come. I heard you ran into some trouble, and I wasn't so sure you'd want an ex-FBI agent around."

"The trouble wasn't exactly my fault."

"I figured."

"You did?"

"Sure. A man can't spend his whole working life in the FBI without being able to tell the good people from the bad. You're one of the good ones."

"Even after what you heard, you kept faith in me?"

"Did you expect me to give more credit to Mason County gossip than to my own instincts?"

"Norman, I can never thank you enough for that," Mamie said, a quaver in her voice.

"It was only natural. Now what can I get you to drink? I have a little hobby here, making my own beer. Would you like to try some?"

We did and found it very good, much lighter and tastier than the typical commercial brews. Norman beamed, and then we settled in as Mamie told him our story. He listened carefully. Afterwards, he asked some questions to make sure he had the facts right. The longer it went, the more his eyes glittered with the look of an old sleuthhound on the case again, especially when Mamie told him about the cockfights.

"I knew about them," Norman said. "I even staked out a few for the hell of it. I saw all the best people of Mason County come and go. There was nothing I could do about it. Raiding them wouldn't have helped, because there would have been so much confusion and so many denials that we never could have made a case. We'd have lost in court, and then they'd have gone back to their cockfighting, laughing at us, cockier than ever, if you'll excuse the pun." He chuckled at his own quip and took a moment to refill our beer glasses. "I needed somebody inside, someone who could infiltrate and be trusted by the Christmases, so I could build up the evidence. But there was never anybody."

"That's what we can do," Mamie said. She sounded excited.

"If I was an active agent, I'd go to work in a minute."

"But can't you still help us?"

"I don't know. Roger Christmas was right — I wouldn't trust any of those local FBI boys now. This would have to go through Washington. I could go up and talk to them, but there's no guarantee, and it could be dangerous for you. Roger probably had the best advice when he told Jess to give it up and leave town."

"We can't, Norman. We just can't. I worked very hard to rebuild my life here with the house and the restaurant, and I'm not going to let her run us out."

Norman sighed. "I know that. Good people just can't walk away and leave the bad to be. I will go to Washington for you, Mamie, and see what I can do. But don't expect miracles. They could turn me down flat. And don't try to contact me again. It's quite possible Senator Christmas will have you two watched. You'll have to wait for me to get back to you, and it could be a long, long time."

It was the best we could do. We left our fate in Norman's hands and headed home.

"I know we don't have much to hope for," Mamie said, "but I can't help feeling better. At least we're doing something. For the first time in years, I don't just feel helpless."

CHAPTER FIFTEEN

Senator began calling me often, if irregularly, with odd jobs she needed done, and I never failed her.

I worked receptions at the Christmas house. I delivered hams or turkeys on Senator's behalf to Mason County families who lost loved ones. I brought in sandwiches from Mamie's restaurant for lunchtime meetings in her office. I answered the telephone one afternoon when Beverly Billingsley had a dentist's appointment. I fetched coffee for Senator and filled up her car with gas. Whatever she wanted, I did.

There was no telling when Senator would call or

how long a job it would be. It didn't matter, even though it meant Mamie and I had to scramble for transportation since we had only the little white Ford between us. About the time Mamie was afraid to ask anyone for another ride, Senator came through with a car leased to her campaign committee, and I drove around in that.

I was paid as irregularly as I worked. Sometimes Senator paid me by the job and sometimes by the week. I never knew when I was getting a check or how much it would be, and I never questioned it. Serfs don't.

Everybody in Mason County knew my past, but there was never so much as a snicker about my return. Crawling back to Senator wasn't an unusual event in these parts. It had happened to much better people than I.

The weeks slipped by, and Mamie and I stopped hoping that every time the phone rang it would be Norman the Terrible — we resigned ourselves to the reality it would be Senator. After about three weeks, I was spending as much time working for her as I was at the restaurant.

One day Senator phoned and asked me to come into the office. Uncharacteristically, she didn't say why.

"Gotta go," I said to Mamie as I hung up the restaurant phone.

"What is it this time?"

"Don't know."

Mamie shrugged. I shrugged back. I took the loaner car and drove in.

It was a surprising time to be summoned, after five-thirty, when the workday was over and the courthouse was quiet except for a couple of deputy sheriffs on duty. I found Senator in her office with Quinton Coombs.

"I've got a special job for you, Jess," she said.

"Sure, Senator."

"It requires a little discretion."

"Haven't you been able to count on me?"

"I wasn't implying otherwise," Senator said, a little bit sharply, and I felt the stinger go in. "Jess, have you ever been to a cockfight?"

There. She had said it. This was the moment I'd been waiting for. I started to sweat.

"Can't say as I have."

Senator cleared her throat. "Every now and then, Mr. Coombs hosts a little match or two at his farm, and I like to help him see it done right. It's a friendly little evening, nothing anyone who isn't invited needs to know about. It makes it nice to have someone there to help out. Would you be willing to do that?"

"When would it be?"

"This Sunday."

I pretended to be surprised. "Sunday? Cockfighting is allowed on Sunday?"

"That's the regular time. After a day of prayer, it's good to start the blood boiling again."

"Sounds all right to me."

"So you can do it?"

"I'm at your service, Senator. You know that."

Mamie and I wished desperately for Norman the Terrible to call so we could tell him I had been hired for a cockfight, but a deal was a deal. We were bound to wait for him to contact us.

"I don't like this," Mamie said. "I don't like you going out there and getting involved in something illegal."

"We knew this might happen. We've done everything we can. We're going to have to play along."

"You'll be entirely at her mercy."

"I'm not already?"

Mamie conceded my point. "All right, you win," she said.

Sunday evening I drove out to the countryside, back to Quinton Coombs' gentleman farm, and eased the little loaner car through the ruts and bumps of dirt paths until I came to a barn. It was a ramshackle old structure with the paint weathered off and boards swaying loose or missing, but that was by design.

Inside it was a different story. The rotting shell concealed a solid roof and strong walls and an honest-to-God amphitheater with rough benches and rails surrounding a cockpit below. I couldn't have been more astonished at the contrast if I had been Alice, falling down the rabbit hole into Wonderland.

It was stifling hot inside, and no amount of cleaning could disguise the faint stench of sweat and decay that clung there and accumulated, cockfight after cockfight. I figured a hospital smelled the same way during the late War of Northern Aggression.

No wonder I didn't have to wear one of those white uniforms for this job. It would have looked ridiculous amid this disrepute. As it was, I felt overdressed in a yellow shirt, worn open at the throat, and a pair of khakis. Mamie was making me get new clothes with some of my money.

Senator had told me to look for a little office off the arena. Its door was open, or I never would have found it. When the door was shut, it blended exactly into the wallboards.

I walked in. Senator was there. The office was furnished with a desk and some filing cabinets and straight-backed chairs, pedestrian enough for a school principal or an accountant. I had trouble detecting the evil.

"Come on in, Jess," Senator said. "You're right on time. Usually I have Mr. Coombs' son and daughter-in-law to help out, but she's pregnant now, which is why I called you in. We're going to keep you hopping tonight. This crowd can get itself pretty worked up. They'll be hollering at you all the time, but don't pay them any mind. Just do what you can."

"All right."

"They'll be betting and they'll be wanting a little something to keep from getting parched. You're to help out. When they want to bet, they'll hand you some money and a betting slip. Run them back to Mr. Coombs. He'll be at a table in the back with me. When they want something to drink, we've got a bar set up with a bartender. They'll tell you what they want, and you go fetch it. They won't be paying — the refreshments are on the house."

"I expect I can handle all that," I said.

"Good. Go introduce yourself to the bartender. His

name's Frank. Ask him if he needs any help setting up. The crowd'll be along soon."

I hustled out and made Frank's acquaintance. Quinton Coombs was already at his table, assembling betting slips and counting the money in a gray metal box. His son Harry was wiping down the benches.

People filtered in, their cheeks ruddy with anticipation. They stopped by Frank's station to pick up drinks and headed for their places as though they had done this many, many times before.

I was staggered by who they were. Among the early entrants were Robert Black III and Royden McGraw, the president and first vice president of the bank where my father had worked. Then came Sam Slaughter, the owner of the print shop, accompanied by old Doc Lelong and his son, who was taking over the practice. They were followed by Hitchens and Mitchem, Esq., the lead partners in the law firm where Mamie's father had been. Hiram Broadbent, the undertaker, showed up, and so did Sheriff Emory, of course. Anybody who was anybody was there — church elders, Rotarians, county commissioners, library trustees. They crammed onto the benches and commenced to cackle.

The amphitheater nearly was filled when Mrs. Letard, the publisher of the *Crier,* and her son Hubert made a grand entrance along with the cages conveying Hubert's prize gamecocks. They were cheered and ushered to seats of honor. Then someone I didn't know came in, leading a whole bunch of other people I'd never laid eyes on. The crowd quit cheering and started jeering, and the newcomers gave it right back.

"Friends! Friends!" Senator called until everyone quieted down.

She threw her arm affectionately across the lead stranger's shoulders. He was handsome, a shade smaller than Senator, with a lady-killer smile, a fine-toned body and dark hair hanging rakishly across his aristocratic forehead.

"As you've all guessed, this is Representative Stuart Morton Claremont from Morton County, my colleague in the state legislature," Senator said.

They gave each other a look that said they were a little bit more than that.

"I've invited him to be with us," Senator went on, "because Representative Claremont tells me he's got the fightingest gamecocks south of the Mason-Dixon line!"

"We'll see about that!" hollered Hiram Broadbent, and the gamesmanship was on.

I was swarmed under with work. Everyone was shouting at the same time, as Senator ordered up the first fight between Representative Claremont's gamecock and one of Sam Slaughter's. I juggled whiskeys, bourbons, beers and rival bets from Mason and Morton counties while sidestepping along the benches past jutting knees.

Just as I brought Doc Lelong's fifty dollars' change from his crisp hundred, the crowd got so loud I paused to watch. Claremont's handler and Slaughter were bringing the birds to the pit and putting the spurs on them.

As soon as the cocks were unhanded, they shrieked and flapped and flung themselves high against the pit walls. Claremont's got higher and came screeching down like a banshee and sunk its spurs into the skull of Slaughter's bird before the poor thing had a chance. Blood arced so fiercely it sprayed the first row, and the gamecock's black eyes went from glittery to flat.

I had never seen death come so starkly. I turned away with a gasp, but I was the only one. The crowd was roaring with the frenzy of a quick kill and laughing at the ones down in front who were brushing the pinpoints of blood on their clothes into muddy streaks.

I'd seen enough. I kept working as the fights went on and a deadly stench made the barn smell like a butcher shop. Once I slipped on some blood and nearly sloshed a beer down Sheriff Emory's back as he leaned excitedly over the rail.

Representative Claremont's birds cut a cruel swath through Mason County's finest. He was making a fortune off hometown pride. Senator let it go on, but she knew what she was doing. At last she called for a match between Claremont and Hubert Letard, and that was that. There wasn't a gamecock born yet that could beat Hubert's.

The crowd went wild when Claremont's bird went down. The representative grinned bravely, but he was clearly unnerved as the Mason County contingent hissed him and whooped and pounded Hubert on the back.

The outworlders were vanquished. They paid their bets and slunk off.

The last drinks were drained. The sated crowd wandered off with Morton County money jingling in its pockets. Quinton Coombs totaled up the house's cut.

“One of the best ever,” he told Senator as he handed her the gray metal box.

I was dead on my feet and dying to be dismissed, but Senator beckoned me over and said, “Will you follow me out to the house?”

“Of course, Senator,” I said.

She smiled.

CHAPTER SIXTEEN

I fought off exhaustion and drove into town. As I stared at the dark windshield, I kept seeing images of the spurs going into that gamecock's head.

Senator's street was so quiet that the sound of her footsteps and mine seemed like an intrusion as we crushed the gravel of her driveway. Her house was the only one with lights on downstairs, although I could see the occasional bedroom light in the homes of the bankers and lawyers and business executives who had been at the cockfights.

Len Buckworth opened the door, and we went inside.

"Evening, Senator," Len said. "Can I get you anything?"

"Not at the moment. We'll be in the library."

I wished I knew what the hell was going on. I followed Senator over thick carpeting into a part of the house I hadn't been to before. We went down a hallway lined with portraits of Christmases past. It was a distinguished gallery of jurists, lawmakers, state Cabinet secretaries and Confederate officers. Hers would be there someday, too.

We entered the family library. It was windowless and oppressive, its floor-to-ceiling bookcases lined with old law books, legislative records and ancient tomes that looked as though they hadn't been opened since Jefferson Davis was president. It was furnished with an elaborate carved desk for Senator, a leather couch and armchairs and a small cart that served as a portable bar.

Senator shut two massive wooden doors guarding the entranceway, making me feel as though I had just been buried alive.

"Have a seat, Jess," said Senator, nodding at the smooth leather couch.

I looked at it dubiously. It was so fine, and I was so grimy, but after a moment I sat anyway.

Senator carried the gray box with the night's profits to her desk and unlatched it. There were wads and wads of bills in there. She picked up a stack and leaned toward the desk lamp to count it. As she bent forward, I could see the high color in her cheeks from the stimulation of the night.

"You did a fine job, Jess, so fine that I wanted to give you a bigger cut than the others are getting."

I watched in surprise as she peeled off four hundred-dollar bills and brought them over. She laid them on a coffee table in front of the couch and sat down next to me. She was so close, she was in Mamie's range. Then I found out why.

Senator put an arm around my shoulder and a hand on my thigh. Her lips nuzzled my cheek. She took her hand from my thigh and unfastened the top buttons of my shirt. *This can't be happening,* I thought, but it was.

She turned my face toward her, and I thought, *I'm going to have to kiss her, and I'm going to have to do whatever else she wants too.*

I needed a miracle to get out of this, and I didn't care what it was — earthquake, fire or a band of angels. I got it.

The sound of voices came from the other side of the door, strident voices raised in disagreement. The handle turned, and Senator bolted up from the couch.

The doors swung open. Roger Christmas stood there, strong-arming Len Buckworth aside. The caretaker fled, without so much as a glance into the library.

Senator glared. Roger smiled gallantly, as though he had not caught us doing what we had been doing.

"Roger! For heaven's sake! What are you doing here?" Senator demanded.

"I've come home," Roger said genially. "I've come home to stay."

"You picked one hell of a time to do it!"

"This is my home too," Roger said mildly. "Hello, Jess, what a surprise to find you here."

I buttoned my shirt and didn't look up.

"Roger," Senator said forcefully, "why don't you go into the parlor, and I'll meet you there in a moment?"

"Sure, Sister, just as soon as I escort Jess to her car."

I didn't need a second invitation. I scrambled from the couch and headed for the door. I left that damned four hundred dollars lying there.

Senator didn't try to stop us. When we were safely outside, Roger said simply, "I'm sorry, Jess. I knew that about my sister, too."

"Roger, don't apologize! How ever did you manage to get here?"

"I meant to arrive sooner. I wanted to be at the cockfight, to head this off, but there was a bridge out, and I had to double back and take a detour."

"But how did you know to come tonight?"

Roger smiled. "I'm not entirely without resources, Jess, and I've been having second thoughts since I last saw you. I know how she takes advantage of people. It's not the gender that matters with her, it's the power. And I know how she gets after cockfights. I couldn't let her do that to you."

"You've given me a whole new appreciation of what it means to arrive in the nick of time."

"Listen, I meant what I said about coming home to stay. I want to see this through with you, and I will do everything in my power to make sure she's never alone with you, cross my heart and hope to die."

"Roger Christmas, you're a new man."

"Never mind that. It's certainly taken me long enough. Do you and Mamie have a plan yet?"

"We think we do."

"Good. We can talk about it another time. Maybe I can help. In the meantime, I think you ought to get home."

He opened the car door for me. As I slid inside, he gave me an affectionate kiss on the cheek. I appreciated it much more than I would have from his sister.

"She did *what?* "

Mamie flew into a fury when I told her what had happened.

"It's all right. Don't make a big deal out of it," I said. All I wanted to do was sag on the porch glider and forget about it.

"I don't have to make a big deal out of it. It's already a big deal. A very big deal," Mamie snapped. She was pacing, looking very prosecutorial.

"Look, just let it go."

"She's not going to get away with this."

"She sure as hell is. What are you going to do about it? Go to Sheriff Emory? Or the county attorney she got elected? How about the judge her father got appointed to the bench? Why don't you go right to the governor and ask him who he wants to side with — Senator Christmas or an ex-con? We're stuck, Mamie. The only way out is to get on with our plan."

"I hate this." Tears of rage and frustration stood in Mamie's eyes.

"I know."

The fight went out of her, and she sat next to me on the glider. We hugged fiercely.

"Suppose she tries again?" Mamie asked.

"Roger will be there."

"Suppose he's not?"

"Mamie, don't ask questions you don't want answered. Believe me, you don't want to know."

CHAPTER SEVENTEEN

Senator didn't call Monday. She didn't call Tuesday or Wednesday either, and I started to worry. Mamie was relieved, but I wasn't. Unless Senator called, we didn't have a chance with our plan, and I really didn't care what it took to do it.

When we opened the restaurant Thursday morning, our first customer was Roger Christmas. He sat at the counter and smiled at us, as gallant as Sir Lancelot.

Mamie looked vastly troubled but then smiled back. I could tell she was thinking about the developments Sunday night but no doubt had decided Roger's virtues outweighed Senator's sins.

"Good morning, Roger," Mamie said. "What'll it be? It's on the house."

"Thank you kindly, Mamie, but there's no need to do that."

"Oh, yes, there is."

"Then just some coffee and a biscuit, please, although I'd be ever so grateful if you had some honey for the biscuit."

"You bet."

Since we were otherwise customerless, I poured myself a cup of coffee and slid onto a stool next to Roger.

"She hasn't called," I said.

"I know. She's been too busy fighting with me. The problem, from her point of view, is I always used to give in, and I'm not this time."

"What are you fighting about?"

"First we fought about me barging in, but we got over that. She admitted the house was as much mine as hers, so I apologized for busting in on her privacy and promised never to do it again. Nothing lost there — I'm sure she'll lock the doors after this."

Roger shook his head and chuckled. Mamie looked grim.

"After we got that out of the way, we moved onto bigger issues," Roger said. "She thinks I'm muscling in, which I am. After all these years, she likes having all the goodies for herself, but she knows she can't make me go away. Father always hoped we would share. It was a disappointment to him when I wouldn't."

"So she's stuck with you," Mamie said.

"It appears so."

"How did you account for your return?" I asked.

"Easy as pie. I told her I heard that Julius Foote, the senior judge at the courthouse, was talking about retiring when his term is up in two years, which is true. I said I was thinking about having his seat for myself, so I figured I ought to come home and get reacquainted with Mason County."

"She bought it?"

"Hard not to. Since she really doesn't want me around, she offered to set me up either in the county attorney's office or in private practice. As a matter of fact, Mamie, she wanted to put me with Hitchens and Mitchem in your father's old firm. But I said no. I said I wanted to work right in the Senate office, to be in the thick of things. She said it didn't work the last time. I said this was different, because I had direction, and anyway, if I wanted to be a judge, I needed to practice more politics than law. I had her there, and she knew it."

"Pretty smooth talking," Mamie said.

"About time I put that law school education to some good use, don't you think? But the important thing is, I'm in a position to do you some good. Can you tell me what your plan is?"

Mamie explained about Norman the Terrible.

Roger listened eagerly. "That sounds like it'll do the trick. I can help, too. I know a lot about those cockfights, and I'm willing to talk. But are you sure he'll come through for you? It's been weeks."

"We're not letting ourselves think about that," Mamie said.

"I see. Well, I better be getting to the courthouse if I want to look serious about this new arrangement.

But count me in. Let me know as soon as you hear from Norman."

Senator finally called for me on the following Tuesday. She had a fruit basket to be delivered to the new president of the Mason County Ladies Christian Temperance League. I hustled out and did it.

The little jobs started coming in again. I took an official autographed senatorial photo to a Boy Scout troop, dropped off her advertising copy for the Mason County Library Association yearbook, delivered a ham to the bereaved Burke family and had a fresh battery put into her wristwatch at the jeweler's. Whatever it took.

My contact with Senator was minimal, sometimes just by telephone. I hoped it would reassure Mamie, but it didn't.

"She's just waiting for the right opportunity," Mamie said.

"Not necessarily," I said, but I was lying. Mamie knew it, and I knew it, and Mamie knew that I knew she knew it.

It was just a matter of time. Senator called and asked me to bring tea sandwiches from the restaurant for an afternoon reception at the courthouse office. She was entertaining the top three finishers from the Mason County Ladies Barbershop Quartet Competition and needed something elegant.

I got the sandwiches and performed the usual chores for the reception. I passed around the food, served coffee and tea and cleaned up the spills. It hadn't dawned on me, though, that this was going to be one of those hazardous-duty assignments. When you have a hot pot of coffee in one hand and a tray with cream and sugar in the other, there is no way to protect yourself from a barbershop singer pinching your cheek with blue-veined fingers.

After a while Mrs. Wormwood, the local piano teacher, winked and said, "You know, Senator, the coffee and tea really hit the spot, but teatime is nearly behind us, and I wonder if you have something a little more stimulating?"

The others fluttered and murmured their agreement, proof there was no overlap between the barbershop quartets and the Mason County Christian Temperance League.

Senator broke out the whiskey. One belt later, the singers' competitive fires were lit, and the quartets got to warbling.

One group was bawling "Good Night, Ladies." Another tuned up with "Row, Row, Row Your Boat." The last went with "Bicycle Built for Two."

It was ghastly. Beverly Billingsley switched the telephone to the answering service and departed, and Quinton Coombs slunk out shortly thereafter. Senator smiled throughout.

Fortunately there were dinners to be served to hungry husbands, and the songfest wound down.

"I must say, Senator," said Mrs. Arnette, and of course she must, "I was a great admirer of your father and very saddened by his premature departure, but we do have such a good time with you!"

They tittered, giggled, hugged Senator and took their leave, blinking their whiskey eyes. Mrs.

Wormwood was still humming "Bicycle Built for Two."

It was late. The courthouse offices were closed. Senator and I were alone.

"The things you do to stay in office," Senator said. Her mood was so good, I immediately started to worry.

"Listen, Jess, I've been thinking. There's going to be another cockfight Sunday night, and I'd like you to work it. But it would be even better if Mamie could come along too and do some catering. Can you arrange that?"

"I believe so, Senator," I said, wondering why she was, in a manner of speaking, upping the ante.

"In the meantime, I've got a job for you tomorrow, Jess. I need you to drive me to the capital in the afternoon. I've got a Finance Committee meeting."

I thought about being alone in the car with her for all those hours, but I said, "Sure, Senator."

"It might run late. There's a possibility we'll have to stay over and drive back in the morning."

Now I understood why Senator was dealing Mamie in, no doubt with handsome compensation. She expected me to make it up to her — alone, overnight, in the capital.

I swallowed. "That's not a problem."

"The General has beautiful rooms. You might want to pack a bag. I'll expect you tomorrow by one o'clock."

Sweet Jesus, I was in a sweat. What the hell was I going to tell Mamie?

It was awful. I drove home and paced the rooms

of our little house, the place where I made love to the only woman I wanted, where every spot we had kissed and touched reproached me as I considered this monstrous tryst with Senator.

I didn't want to tell Mamie the truth. I thought I'd tell her I was driving Senator up for the afternoon, and then I'd call her from the capital to say we had been delayed. It would be a done deed, nothing anyone could do anything about.

Mamie would know, though. When I told her we were driving up, she would read in my eyes there was more to it. She would catch me in the lie. Then how would it be?

I didn't know which was worse, telling the truth or telling a lie.

Mamie's car was turning into the driveway. I was out of time to decide.

The telephone rang, and I answered it.

"Hello, Jess? This is Roger Christmas. I've just learned of my sister's schedule for tomorrow. I told her I'd be happy to drive her to the meeting. She won't be needing you after all."

"Roger, you are truly a guardian angel."

"Hey, I promised, didn't I?"

I hung up before Mamie got in. Once again the cavalry had come over the hill, just when it was needed the most.

I greeted Mamie with a passionate kiss.

"You're in an awful good mood," she teased.

"You would be too if you'd just had the afternoon I did. Say, Mamie, have you ever heard 'Good Night, Ladies,' 'Row, Row, Row Your Boat' and 'Bicycle Built for Two' all bellowed at the same time?"

"Can't say as I have."

"And have you ever had Mrs. Arnette pinch your cheek?"

"No, not that either."

"Well, I have. That's what happened this afternoon."

"And that put you in a good mood?"

"Hell, no! Having it stop did."

Mamie laughed. I laughed. Then I took her hand and headed for the bedroom. Dodging bullets can make you feel that way. No wonder there are so many army brats in the world.

CHAPTER EIGHTEEN

Mamie was reluctant to go to the cockfight, but she knew she had to do it. On Sunday she prepared turkey and ham and some three-bean salad, cooked up a mess of cornbread and swore an uncharacteristic blue streak the whole time. I watched baseball games on television and stayed out of her way.

"The only way I'm getting through this," she grumbled, "is by remembering it can put her in jail."

"That's the idea," I said.

It was also the idea that we needed Norman the Terrible to put her there, and time was passing without a peep from him. Neither one of us mentioned it, though.

We loaded up Mamie's car and drove out to Quinton Coombs' farm. I helped Mamie set up her table next to Frank the bartender. While we were working, Senator came in and cast an approving eye at Mamie's handiwork. Better she should look at Mamie's food that way than at me.

"That's a real nice spread, Mamie," Senator said. "Why don't you take a break for a minute and join me in the office?"

They were gone a long time. I got a Coke from Frank and cooled my heels. When Mamie finally returned, she had a funny look on her face, and we walked off to a corner to talk.

"What's the matter?" I asked.

"Nothing. She likes my work."

"So why are you looking like something's wrong?"

"She wants to put me on a monthly retainer to handle all of her senatorial receptions. She says I should consider setting up a catering business in Mason City, and she can fix it that I get the business for the Rotary and the Lions and the garden clubs and the church socials and so forth. She says it would be a lot less work than the restaurant, and the money would be better."

"Back across the county line, into her territory."

"Precisely."

"What did you tell her?"

"Well, I couldn't very well turn down the retainer, could I? She's talking a thousand a month. I told her the catering business would take some more thought, and anyway, I had contracts to honor at the restaurant. She laughed and said we both had been to law school, and we knew there wasn't a contract written that couldn't be broken. She said she'd ask Roger to look into it, since he was the real lawyer in the family, and figure it out."

"She's used to having her own way."

"I can see why."

"And we're getting in deeper and deeper."

"I wish this was over. I guarantee you, I'll be making mental notes tonight in earnest. I want this to stick."

As the sun set, the locals filtered in. They exclaimed in surprise over Mamie's fixings and helped themselves to generous portions. On most matters they were conservative, but they clearly were liberal when it came to food.

Mamie managed to look most of them in the eye and smile, but she couldn't manage it with Hitchens and Mitchem, Esq., her father's old law partners. They had been good to her in her youth, but now she saw them for what they were. She turned away and wiped her hands on a towel, and I felt bad for her.

The mood was festive this evening, a little more freewheeling and manic than the last time, because this was an all-Mason County affair. There would be no guest gladiators from beyond our borders.

Roger wandered in just before the first cockfight and joined his sister from her vantage point behind the arena. He smiled and nodded and was friendly enough, but it was clearly Senator's show.

I was glad to see him. With both Roger and Mamie there, I figured I was safe from Senator for the night.

Sam Slaughter, the printer, got everyone going.

"Got me a new bird," he bragged. "Got it from a breeder out of Kentucky, where the only thing finer than their bourbon is their birds. Anyone here brave enough to try?"

"I bet that bird's like you, all squawk and talk," said Arnie Brummer, one of Billy Emory's deputy sheriffs.

"Did you bring a bird tonight, Arnie?" Senator asked.

"Don't you know it, Senator," Arnie answered.

"Then let's have at it."

Slaughter whooped and chugged a beer and headed for the ring, while Arnie cooed to his bird as though it were a baby. I got busy hustling bets up to Senator's table and bringing back booze.

The crowd was loud and demanding, and I had trouble shoving through. There was no hope of keeping up with the demand. Once I leaned down a row to hand the president-elect of the Mason County Rotary Club his shot of whiskey, and someone took the opportunity to make a rude grab at my breast. I didn't look to see who it was, because I didn't want to know, and I never made the mistake of stretching out again. There was no telling how many of the people here got overstimulated by cockfighting. I already knew about Senator and now this touchy-feely Mysterious Stranger, and that was enough.

Slaughter's and Arnie's birds had at it just as I delivered a whiskey to Hiram Broadbent, the undertaker, perched in the front row. I got trapped there against the rail as the crowd surged forward for a look.

Slaughter's bird screeched as it was wounded. It flew up flapping, spraying blood everywhere, and I was spattered. The wound wasn't mortal, though, and the gamecock moved back in. It sunk its spurs into the neck of Arnie's bird, and the first match was over.

In disgust I fought my way out of the crush and back to Mamie. She was pale.

"I hope you have another shirt to change into," she said.

"I don't."

"This is brutal."

"That bird's no deader than your turkey is."

"This turkey gave up its life for a good cause."

"These people think that bird did, too." Mamie glared, and I backed off. "Hey, I was just kidding," I said.

"I don't know how you can kid about this."

It was a very long night. I was beat by the end of it and half-sick from the stench of sweat and spilled beer and slaughter. Mamie and I walked out into the steam heat and didn't say a word to each other. I didn't know whether she was upset with Senator or me, and I didn't necessarily want to find out.

The silence didn't last long. There was a black Oldsmobile parked in our driveway. Norman the Terrible had returned, and best of all, he was smiling.

"I tailed you tonight," he said, a look in his eye like a man who just had filled an inside straight. "It was an unofficial one-man stakeout, just for practice. The FBI is coming in."

"Norman, I knew you'd come through!" Mamie said.

They hugged joyfully, and we went inside.

"I'm sorry it took so long," Norman said. "Washington was interested right away, but you know how the government works. You can't just leave a field operation to the field agents. The brass has to be briefed, and the budget analysts brought in and the attorneys from the Justice Department. Then just when you think it's all wrapped up, somebody important goes on vacation, and you can't get a signature and you have to wait some more."

Mamie nodded sympathetically. "I know. Much as I miss being a prosecutor, I don't miss all that government red tape."

"Well, we're ready now. A couple of agents should be here in two or three weeks. You'll be interviewed, and we'll stake out the cockfights, and some IRS guys will be brought in to look at Senator Christmas's finances. I'm happy to say I've been activated for this little operation. As a matter of fact, I'll be your main contact. I'm still leery of the phone, so I'll just stop by the restaurant every now and then. Okay?"

"Norman, you're a miracle worker," Mamie said.

"If I am, then you're the miracle. We don't often have informants like the two of you."

I didn't much like the sound of that. "Isn't *informant* just a high-toned word for *snitch?* "

"One person's snitch is another person's hero," Norman said. "In this case, it's better to snitch on Senator Christmas and be a hero to the FBI. It will keep you out of jail."

"I snitched on Senator the last time, and I went to jail."

"We'll try to get it right this time, okay?"

"I suppose."

CHAPTER NINETEEN

Mamie and I were ecstatic — until Tuesday. That was the day Senator called me into her office and told me to shut the door.

"I don't usually like to have cockfights two Sundays in a row," she said, "but the customers are clamoring for it. I think Mamie's table is a big reason why. Do you think she can turn around and do it again?"

"Sure, Senator," I said, although I was reluctant.

I was hoping there wouldn't be any more Sundays until the new FBI agents came to town.

"That's the spirit. By the way, I'm expecting the audit on Mamie's restaurant to come down any day now from the State Bureau of Revenue. I sure hope it goes well, don't you?"

"Yes, Senator, I do," I said, trying not to look too wary. Something was up. Senator and I both knew the audit would turn out exactly the way she wanted it to.

"I just had an idea, Jess. Maybe there's something we can do to help."

"What's that, Senator?"

"Let's you and me drive up to the capital and pay a visit on the director of revenue, just to see how things are going. We'll make an appointment for Monday morning. We'll leave right after the cockfight Sunday night and stay over. What do you say?"

I couldn't breathe. Suddenly I knew just how a fish felt, flopping on the fetid bottom of a boat with the hook still in it.

I was getting this message loud and clear. Either I put out, or the audit would ruin Mamie, and heaven knows what else Senator would come up with.

Well, it was only one night. The FBI would get her in the end.

"Sure, Senator. It'll be like a holiday."

Some holiday. Sort of like commemorating Lee's surrender at Appomattox.

Mamie was going to kill me for this.

* * * * *

I had to tell her. I rehearsed different lines all the way home as I drove the rental car that Senator had provided for me in that display of her ubiquitous reach.

Eventually I realized there was no way to sugarcoat this, so I didn't bother. I told Mamie straight out what Senator wanted.

"We have to go through with it," I said. "We have to keep her thinking she's totally in control. We're too close to the end to have this fall apart — for anything."

Mamie's eyes fired with that prosecutor's look, which always seemed to be lurking somewhere these days. She glared at me as though I were a murderer who had gotten off.

"Get in the car," she snapped.

"It's late. Where are we going?"

"Norman's."

"Mamie, he said he'd stop by the restaurant. I'm not sure we should risk these trips."

"Come on, Jess. Or do you want to sleep with her? Is that what this is all about?"

That hurt pretty much, but I knew when to keep my mouth shut. I headed for the car.

Mamie wasn't talking. After three or four miles, I put my hand on her thigh but she ignored me. I pulled back, closed my eyes and just tried to float along, emotion washing through me like waves of seasickness. I was in so far over my head, I didn't know what to do.

I roused myself when I felt the car turn off the macadam onto the dusty road leading to Norman's cottage. His lights blazed in the distance. Mamie slowed to ease the car over the bumpy surface.

“Mamie, don’t be mad,” I pleaded.

“I am mad. I’m furious as hell at her, and I have every right to be. But I’m not mad at you. I’m sorry if it seems that way. I just get so singleminded.”

She stopped the car abruptly. “Hey.” She drew me over and kissed me tenderly. It trickled through me like a warm drink.

We sat in the car, parked in the road out in the middle of nowhere, and made out like a couple of high school sweethearts. I slipped my hand under her shirt and teased her nipples the way she liked it. She squirmed in her seat and pressed her lips against mine.

The danger, sitting out there in the open, was exquisite. Mamie finally broke it off with a sigh. “This is a hell of a way to go chasing criminals.”

“I always wondered what prosecutors got out of it.”

Mamie giggled and swatted me good-naturedly. We rearranged our clothes and ourselves as best we could by the rearview mirror and the dashboard light.

Mamie drove the last stretch to the cottage. Norman looked concerned when he answered Mamie’s knock and looked around before letting us in.

“You need to be doing as little as possible that might arouse suspicion,” he said. “Do you think you were followed?”

“I’m sure we weren’t,” Mamie said.

If we were, they got quite a show, I thought.

“I’m sorry, Norman, but it’s an emergency,” Mamie said. “You’ve got to rethink the operation. You’ve got to do the raid this Sunday.”

“Mamie, it’s Tuesday night. That’s five days from now. The agents aren’t due in town for a couple weeks. You know that. Then we've got to interview you and Jess and talk to Roger Christmas, and we've got to get warrants and stake out the cockfights and bring in the IRS and coordinate with the U.S. attorney. It can't happen overnight."

"It's got to. Either you move in Sunday, or Jess and I will have to pull out. It's now or never."

"Hold on there. This was your idea. I've gone to considerable trouble to set this up. I put my reputation on the line for you, and now you're threatening to back out?"

"We're not backing out. I just want it speeded up, that's all."

"Do you know how good the chances are we'll blow this if we move that fast?"

"I'm telling you, it's that fast or nothing."

"Mamie, what's driving you? What's the matter?"

"I can't tell you. It's personal."

Norman sighed in deep exasperation. "You want me to do this and you can't even tell me why?"

"That's right."

"This is out of the question. This is nuts."

Mamie and Norman stared at each other, showdown in their eyes. I didn't know whether to bet on Mamie leaving, dragging me out with her, or Norman throwing us out. Either way, our little scheme was done for — and so were we.

Norman's eyes softened first and then Mamie's. They looked less like a couple of boxers and more like a father and daughter, and I hadn't met a father yet who would let his daughter down when she looked like that.

"You're asking the impossible," Norman said, "but I'll see what I can do. I can't make you any promises, and I definitely can't be in contact with you. You two go to the cockfight on Sunday night. If I show up, I show up. If not, that's the breaks."

"Oh, Norman, I knew you'd understand," Mamie said.

"Actually, I don't understand, and I'm terribly afraid it can't be done. But if this is the way you want it . . ."

"I do."

CHAPTER TWENTY

Not in the days after I was arrested by the State Bureau of Investigation, not in the days after I learned my folks had died within weeks of each other, did the time drag the way it did as we waited for the Sunday night cockfight.

Mamie and I didn't speak very much. Although I was never one for naps, I took one every chance I got. I found myself glancing at clocks and calendars — as if that would help.

I wanted to ask Mamie what we would do if Norman and the FBI didn't show. Did I go with

Senator to the capital, or did Mamie and I fly out of there, conceding defeat, and keep on going?

I didn't ask, though. I was pretty sure she would just tell me to trust Norman and not worry about the hypotheticals.

When Sunday evening finally labored in, I went to the bedroom to pack an overnight bag. Mamie was right behind me.

"What are you doing?"

"Packing."

"Why are you doing that?"

"To make it look good."

"You're not going to need it."

"I don't expect I am. I just want to have it in case Senator asks, that's all."

"Norman is coming."

"Sure he is, and the South will rise again. I'm just not ready to get out my Confederate money yet, that's all."

Mamie wasn't happy, but she let it go. I was finished in a minute, and then we loaded up the car and headed for Quinton Coombs' farm. This was it, payback or nothing.

When we arrived, I took my bag and went to Senator's office. It was a good thing I knew where the door was, because it was devilishly hard to find.

I knocked, Senator answered and I let myself in. She looked delighted when she saw the bag.

"Evening, Jess. All set for tonight."

"Can't wait, Senator," I said, and I was being truthful. Never mind that we were planning two different events.

I went out to help Mamie. Frank the bartender came in and set up beside us. Then Roger made a surprise early appearance and walked over to say hello.

"Jess, Mamie, everything looks great. I see it's ham and turkey again. Well, it sure was a hit last time," he said.

"I'd change the menu, but I just couldn't bring myself to do chicken," Mamie said.

"What's the matter, Mamie?" Frank the bartender asked. "Those gamecocks have about as much in common with fried chicken as ham does with hamburger."

"Or sand with sandwiches," Roger said.

"Stop it," Mamie said. "Next thing you all will be telling me you don't need barking dogs to make hush puppies."

I didn't know where Mamie's high spirits were coming from, but I sure was proud of her. I couldn't wait for this night to be over.

Roger wandered off and I whispered to Mamie, "I think I better tell Roger about tonight."

Mamie nodded and I quickly waylaid him. In a low voice I said, "Norman the Terrible and his friends may be coming."

Roger looked stricken. "What, stakeout or raid?"

"Raid."

"Sweet Jesus. You didn't tell me it was happening so fast."

"It might not, but I think it will."

"I've got to think about this. I'm not sure I want to be here when it happens." He hurried from the barn.

Well, it was up to him where he wanted to be. He had helped us so much already.

The regulars began arriving shortly, descending

greedily on Mamie's table and packing onto the benches around the pit. I was so keyed up I delivered Doc Lelong's double bourbon instead of a ladylike gin-and-tonic to Mrs. Letard, but it worked out. She knocked it back without blinking before I could apologize.

"Mrs. Letard, I'm sorry. I believe I brought you the wrong drink."

"Oh my goodness! So you did, dear, and I've gone and finished it. Well, mistakes do happen. Just bring me my G-and-T, and we won't say another word about it, will we?"

Mrs. Letard smiled and handed me a tip. No wonder you couldn't believe what you read in her newspaper. She was a living, breathing cover-up herself.

The designated villain for the evening was a banking lobbyist named Reed Hathaway, who brought along his gamecocks and a bunch of well-heeled bankers to bet against Mason County's finest. They fawned all over Senator, said insulting things to the locals and couldn't wait to start throwing their money around. Once again cockfighting helped to remind me that tackiness knew no class.

One fight into the evening Roger showed up again. He gave me the briefest of glances, which I couldn't read, and went to stand by his sister. I watched him for any signs of anxiety that could tip her off to trouble, but he seemed relaxed enough as he chatted with her, occasionally whispering close to her ear, and the night wore on.

Fight followed fight until we reached the point where Senator could shut it down at any time. From the lower benches I caught her staring at me instead of the gamecocks screeching below. I looked in desperation at Mamie, who shrugged. There was no sign of the FBI, and I guessed the jig was up.

Reed's best bird took out Hubert Letard's, and it was clear Mason County's wouldn't be staying home tonight. The bankers were hooting and getting richer, and Senator was going to have to call it off to stop the drain on local pride and pockets.

"Folks," she said, and then we heard the sound of pounding feet. The barn door slammed open.

"FBI! Don't anybody move!" shouted an amplified voice.

The air filled with curses and screams. The crowd ran for its life, overturning benches, spilling drinks, flailing uselessly against the walls and surging futilely against the only exit, where the federal agents were making their stand.

I was knocked about in the crush. Something cracked so hard against my ribs it took my breath away. I got wise and fought my way down toward the pit, while everyone else fled up, so I could see what was going on.

Mamie was behind her table, which shielded her from the crowd. I saw Roger scoop up the gray metal box with the night's take and all the records. He grabbed Senator's hand, and they disappeared into her office behind the camouflage of the door.

Norman the Terrible, as gallant as a knight, shoved his way in and made for Mamie's table. I pushed to join them. Around me the resistance was lessening as the crowd realized it was done for. Already you could see the expressions of panic change to the wounded looks of outraged citizens who would be demanding to see their lawyers. Of course, many of their lawyers were already there.

I reached Mamie and Norman. He gave the game away by hugging us both. People were pointing, but I didn't care. We were safe, safe, safe, and we had won.

"Where is she?" Norman said.

"In her office," I said.

"Where? I can't see it."

"I know. It's disguised. Follow me."

I showed him. "Stay back," he ordered, drew his gun and flung open the door.

There was no one inside.

Senator's desk had been moved. Where it had stood there now gaped the opening of a trap door, revealing a carefully constructed escape tunnel.

"Well, I'll be," Norman the Terrible said.

Norman drove us hundreds of miles that night to a safe house out of state and left us with an FBI agent to protect us. He said he would return as soon as he could.

The house had a pretty decent library, so we passed the time mostly by reading, Mamie with a John Grisham and me with Rita Mae Brown. Mamie also cooked a lot, which she said always steadied her nerves. Jerome, the FBI agent, said he had never had an assignment in which he had eaten so well.

Norman was back by Thursday.

"The Christmases got away," he said. "We followed the tunnel to where it came out in some woods. It must have been there for years as insurance against a raid. We found four-wheel-drive tire tracks in the woods near the tunnel exit, so they obviously had a vehicle waiting for them. They drove right to the county airfield and were out of there on a private jet even before we had a bulletin out on the four-wheel-drive."

"This is impossible," I said.

"Their bank accounts were cleaned out, and their passports are gone. They could be anywhere, and they have more than enough money to hold out comfortably for the rest of their lives."

"How could this have happened?" Mamie asked.

"Roger Christmas. It looks as though he wasn't quite the friend you thought he was. Ever since he returned, he's been methodically preparing for flight. All he needed was the word from you on when to fly. I'd say he put the finishing touches on it when he left you before the cockfights Sunday night. Then all he had to do was grab his sister and go."

Mamie and I looked at each other in disbelief.

"I'd like to give him the benefit of the doubt," I said. "I'd like to think he truly wanted to stop her, but he didn't have the heart to turn her over to the FBI."

"We always said he was a reluctant Christmas. But in the end, he was still a Christmas," Mamie said.

"Well, the FBI thinks of him as a fugitive from justice," Norman said. We thought about that gravely for a moment, and then Norman said, "Of course, the FBI thinks you two are heroes, and we're prepared to help you any way we can. Have you given any thought to what you want to do now?"

"I don't expect we can go back to Mason County," Mamie said drily.

"Probably not a good idea," Norman said, "particularly since we may not even press charges against anybody for the cockfighting. It was Senator Christmas we wanted for corruption, and not that penny-ante stuff. It's hardly worth the effort, since Roger got away with all the records and everybody is lying to protect everybody else."

"So they're going to get away with it," Mamie said.

"Afraid so. I hear Sheriff Emory is already campaigning for the Senate seat in the event it's declared vacant, which of course it will be. He'll just step in where she left off."

"This is so unfair," I said.

"A good deed is its own punishment," Norman said.

"The hell with Mason County," Mamie said. "I'm ready to try something new. Maybe north, maybe west, I don't care. Norman, now that the truth is out, do you suppose the FBI could help me get my law license back?"

"I think that's possible," Norman said. "We can also sell your restaurant and house for you. That should be a nice nest egg."

"I'd be grateful," Mamie said. She looked at me. "Jess, what do you want to do?"

"I don't know. I haven't really thought about it."

"That is so like you," Mamie said, but affectionately.

"I know what," I said. "Maybe I could take up writing again. Maybe even get back into newspaper."

"It sounds good to me," Norman said, smiling. "You won't need the FBI's help for that."

"Don't be too sure, Norman. Haven't you ever heard of anonymous sources?"

"Anonymous source? Isn't that just a high-toned word for *snitch?* "

"Very funny, Norman."

We laughed and laughed. We were going to be just fine.

A few of the publications of

THE NAIAD PRESS, INC.
P.O. Box 10543 • Tallahassee, Florida 32302
Phone (904) 539-5965
Toll-Free Order Number: 1-800-533-1973
Mail orders welcome. Please include 15% postage.

PAXTON COURT by Diane Salvatore. 256 pp. Erotic and wickedly funny contemporary tale about the business of learning to live together.	ISBN 1-56280-109-0	$10.95
PAYBACK by Celia Cohen. 176 pp. A gripping thriller of romance, revenge and betrayal.	ISBN 1-56280-084-1	10.95
THE BEACH AFFAIR by Barbara Johnson. 224 pp. Sizzling summer romance/mystery/intrigue.	ISBN 1-56280-090-6	10.95
GETTING THERE by Robbi Sommers. 192 pp. Nobody does it like Robbi!	ISBN 1-56280-099-X	10.95
FINAL CUT by Lisa Haddock. 208 pp. 2nd Carmen Ramirez mystery.	ISBN 1-56280-088-4	10.95
FLASHPOINT by Katherine V. Forrest. 256 pp. A Lesbian blockbuster!	ISBN 1-56280-079-5	10.95
DAUGHTERS OF A CORAL DAWN by Katherine V. Forrest. Audio Book — read by Jane Merrow.	ISBN 1-56280-110-4	16.95
CLAIRE OF THE MOON by Nicole Conn. Audio Book —Read by Marianne Hyatt.	ISBN 1-56280-113-9	16.95
FOR LOVE AND FOR LIFE: INTIMATE PORTRAITS OF LESBIAN COUPLES by Susan Johnson. 224 pp.	ISBN 1-56280-091-4	14.95
DEVOTION by Mindy Kaplan. 192 pp. See the movie — read the book!	ISBN 1-56280-093-0	10.95
SOMEONE TO WATCH by Jaye Maiman. 272 pp. A Robin Miller mystery. 4th in a series.	ISBN 1-56280-095-7	10.95
GREENER THAN GRASS by Jennifer Fulton. 208 pp. A young woman — a stranger in her bed.	ISBN 1-56280-092-2	10.95
TRAVELS WITH DIANA HUNTER by Regine Sands. Erotic lesbian romp. Audio Book (2 cassettes)	ISBN 1-56280-107-4	16.95
CABIN FEVER by Carol Schmidt. 256 pp. Sizzling suspense and passion.	ISBN 1-56280-089-1	10.95
THERE WILL BE NO GOODBYES by Laura DeHart Young. 192 pp. Romantic love, strength, and friendship.	ISBN 1-56280-103-1	10.95

FAULTLINE by Sheila Ortiz Taylor. 144 pp. Joyous comic lesbian novel. ISBN 1-56280-108-2 9.95

OPEN HOUSE by Pat Welch. 176 pp. P.I. Helen Black's fourth case. ISBN 1-56280-102-3 10.95

ONCE MORE WITH FEELING by Peggy J. Herring. 240 pp. Lighthearted, loving romantic adventure. ISBN 1-56280-089-2 10.95

FOREVER by Evelyn Kennedy. 224 pp. Passionate romance — love overcoming all obstacles. ISBN 1-56280-094-9 10.95

WHISPERS by Kris Bruyer. 176 pp. Romantic ghost story ISBN 1-56280-082-5 10.95

NIGHT SONGS by Penny Mickelbury. 224 pp. A Gianna Maglione Mystery. Second in a series. ISBN 1-56280-097-3 10.95

GETTING TO THE POINT by Teresa Stores. 256 pp. Classic southern Lesbian novel. ISBN 1-56280-100-7 10.95

PAINTED MOON by Karin Kallmaker. 224 pp. Delicious Kallmaker romance. ISBN 1-56280-075-2 10.95

THE MYSTERIOUS NAIAD edited by Katherine V. Forrest & Barbara Grier. 320 pp. Love stories by Naiad Press authors. ISBN 1-56280-074-4 14.95

DAUGHTERS OF A CORAL DAWN by Katherine V. Forrest. 240 pp. Tenth Anniversay Edition. ISBN 1-56280-104-X 10.95

BODY GUARD by Claire McNab. 208 pp. A Carol Ashton Mystery. 6th in a series. ISBN 1-56280-073-6 10.95

CACTUS LOVE by Lee Lynch. 192 pp. Stories by the beloved storyteller. ISBN 1-56280-071-X 9.95

SECOND GUESS by Rose Beecham. 216 pp. An Amanda Valentine Mystery. 2nd in a series. ISBN 1-56280-069-8 9.95

THE SURE THING by Melissa Hartman. 208 pp. L.A. earthquake romance. ISBN 1-56280-078-7 9.95

A RAGE OF MAIDENS by Lauren Wright Douglas. 240 pp. A Caitlin Reece Mystery. 6th in a series. ISBN 1-56280-068-X 10.95

TRIPLE EXPOSURE by Jackie Calhoun. 224 pp. Romantic drama involving many characters. ISBN 1-56280-067-1 9.95

UP, UP AND AWAY by Catherine Ennis. 192 pp. Delightful romance. ISBN 1-56280-065-5 9.95

PERSONAL ADS by Robbi Sommers. 176 pp. Sizzling short stories. ISBN 1-56280-059-0 9.95

FLASHPOINT by Katherine V. Forrest. 256 pp. Lesbian blockbuster! ISBN 1-56280-043-4 22.95

CROSSWORDS by Penny Sumner. 256 pp. 2nd Victoria Cross Mystery. ISBN 1-56280-064-7 9.95

SWEET CHERRY WINE by Carol Schmidt. 224 pp. A novel of suspense. ISBN 1-56280-063-9 9.95

CERTAIN SMILES by Dorothy Tell. 160 pp. Erotic short stories. ISBN 1-56280-066-3 9.95

EDITED OUT by Lisa Haddock. 224 pp. 1st Carmen Ramirez Mystery. ISBN 1-56280-077-9 9.95

WEDNESDAY NIGHTS by Camarin Grae. 288 pp. Sexy adventure. ISBN 1-56280-060-4 10.95

SMOKEY O by Celia Cohen. 176 pp. Relationships on the playing field. ISBN 1-56280-057-4 9.95

KATHLEEN O'DONALD by Penny Hayes. 256 pp. Rose and Kathleen find each other and employment in 1909 NYC. ISBN 1-56280-070-1 9.95

STAYING HOME by Elisabeth Nonas. 256 pp. Molly and Alix want a baby . . . or do they? ISBN 1-56280-076-0 10.95

TRUE LOVE by Jennifer Fulton. 240 pp. Six lesbians searching for love in all the "right" places. ISBN 1-56280-035-3 10.95

GARDENIAS WHERE THERE ARE NONE by Molleen Zanger. 176 pp. Why is Melanie inextricably drawn to the old house? ISBN 1-56280-056-6 9.95

KEEPING SECRETS by Penny Mickelbury. 208 pp. A Gianna Maglione Mystery. First in a series. ISBN 1-56280-052-3 9.95

THE ROMANTIC NAIAD edited by Katherine V. Forrest & Barbara Grier. 336 pp. Love stories by Naiad Press authors. ISBN 1-56280-054-X 14.95

UNDER MY SKIN by Jaye Maiman. 336 pp. A Robin Miller mystery. 3rd in a series. ISBN 1-56280-049-3. 10.95

STAY TOONED by Rhonda Dicksion. 144 pp. Cartoons — 1st collection since *Lesbian Survival Manual.* ISBN 1-56280-045-0 9.95

CAR POOL by Karin Kallmaker. 272pp. Lesbians on wheels and then some! ISBN 1-56280-048-5 10.95

NOT TELLING MOTHER: STORIES FROM A LIFE by Diane Salvatore. 176 pp. Her 3rd novel. ISBN 1-56280-044-2 9.95

GOBLIN MARKET by Lauren Wright Douglas. 240pp. A Caitlin Reece Mystery. 5th in a series. ISBN 1-56280-047-7 10.95

LONG GOODBYES by Nikki Baker. 256 pp. A Virginia Kelly mystery. 3rd in a series. ISBN 1-56280-042-6 9.95

FRIENDS AND LOVERS by Jackie Calhoun. 224 pp. Mid-western Lesbian lives and loves. ISBN 1-56280-041-8 10.95

THE CAT CAME BACK by Hilary Mullins. 208 pp. Highly praised Lesbian novel. ISBN 1-56280-040-X 9.95

BEHIND CLOSED DOORS by Robbi Sommers. 192 pp. Hot, erotic short stories. ISBN 1-56280-039-6 9.95

CLAIRE OF THE MOON by Nicole Conn. 192 pp. See the movie — read the book! ISBN 1-56280-038-8 10.95

SILENT HEART by Claire McNab. 192 pp. Exotic Lesbian romance. ISBN 1-56280-036-1 10.95

HAPPY ENDINGS by Kate Brandt. 272 pp. Intimate conversations with Lesbian authors. ISBN 1-56280-050-7 10.95

THE SPY IN QUESTION by Amanda Kyle Williams. 256 pp. 4th Madison McGuire. ISBN 1-56280-037-X 9.95

SAVING GRACE by Jennifer Fulton. 240 pp. Adventure and romantic entanglement. ISBN 1-56280-051-5 9.95

THE YEAR SEVEN by Molleen Zanger. 208 pp. Women surviving in a new world. ISBN 1-56280-034-5 9.95

CURIOUS WINE by Katherine V. Forrest. 176 pp. Tenth Anniversary Edition. The most popular contemporary Lesbian love story. ISBN 1-56280-053-1 10.95

Audio Book (2 cassettes) ISBN 1-56280-105-8 16.95

CHAUTAUQUA by Catherine Ennis. 192 pp. Exciting, romantic adventure. ISBN 1-56280-032-9 9.95

A PROPER BURIAL by Pat Welch. 192 pp. A Helen Black mystery. 3rd in a series. ISBN 1-56280-033-7 9.95

SILVERLAKE HEAT: A Novel of Suspense by Carol Schmidt. 240 pp. Rhonda is as hot as Laney's dreams. ISBN 1-56280-031-0 9.95

LOVE, ZENA BETH by Diane Salvatore. 224 pp. The most talked about lesbian novel of the nineties! ISBN 1-56280-030-2 10.95

A DOORYARD FULL OF FLOWERS by Isabel Miller. 160 pp. Stories incl. 2 sequels to *Patience and Sarah.* ISBN 1-56280-029-9 9.95

MURDER BY TRADITION by Katherine V. Forrest. 288 pp. A Kate Delafield Mystery. 4th in a series. ISBN 1-56280-002-7 10.95

THE EROTIC NAIAD edited by Katherine V. Forrest & Barbara Grier. 224 pp. Love stories by Naiad Press authors. ISBN 1-56280-026-4 13.95

DEAD CERTAIN by Claire McNab. 224 pp. A Carol Ashton mystery. 5th in a series. ISBN 1-56280-027-2 9.95

CRAZY FOR LOVING by Jaye Maiman. 320 pp. A Robin Miller mystery. 2nd in a series. ISBN 1-56280-025-6 9.95

STONEHURST by Barbara Johnson. 176 pp. Passionate regency romance. ISBN 1-56280-024-8 10.95

INTRODUCING AMANDA VALENTINE by Rose Beecham. 256 pp. An Amanda Valentine Mystery. First in a series. ISBN 1-56280-021-3 9.95

UNCERTAIN COMPANIONS by Robbi Sommers. 204 pp.
Steamy, erotic novel. ISBN 1-56280-017-5 9.95

A TIGER'S HEART by Lauren W. Douglas. 240 pp. A Caitlin
Reece mystery. 4th in a series. ISBN 1-56280-018-3 9.95

PAPERBACK ROMANCE by Karin Kallmaker. 256 pp. A
delicious romance. ISBN 1-56280-019-1 9.95

MORTON RIVER VALLEY by Lee Lynch. 304 pp. Lee Lynch
at her best! ISBN 1-56280-016-7 9.95

THE LAVENDER HOUSE MURDER by Nikki Baker. 224 pp.
A Virginia Kelly Mystery. 2nd in a series. ISBN 1-56280-012-4 9.95

PASSION BAY by Jennifer Fulton. 224 pp. Passionate romance,
virgin beaches, tropical skies. ISBN 1-56280-028-0 10.95

STICKS AND STONES by Jackie Calhoun. 208 pp. Contemporary
lesbian lives and loves. ISBN 1-56280-020-5 9.95
Audio Book (2 cassettes) ISBN 1-56280-106-6 16.95

DELIA IRONFOOT by Jeane Harris. 192 pp. Adventure for Delia
and Beth in the Utah mountains. ISBN 1-56280-014-0 9.95

UNDER THE SOUTHERN CROSS by Claire McNab. 192 pp.
Romantic nights Down Under. ISBN 1-56280-011-6 9.95

GRASSY FLATS by Penny Hayes. 256 pp. Lesbian romance in
the '30s. ISBN 1-56280-010-8 9.95

A SINGULAR SPY by Amanda K. Williams. 192 pp. 3rd
Madison McGuire. ISBN 1-56280-008-6 8.95

THE END OF APRIL by Penny Sumner. 240 pp. A Victoria
Cross mystery. First in a series. ISBN 1-56280-007-8 8.95

HOUSTON TOWN by Deborah Powell. 208 pp. A Hollis
Carpenter mystery. ISBN 1-56280-006-X 8.95

KISS AND TELL by Robbi Sommers. 192 pp. Scorching stories
by the author of *Pleasures.* ISBN 1-56280-005-1 10.95

STILL WATERS by Pat Welch. 208 pp. A Helen Black mystery.
2nd in a series. ISBN 0-941483-97-5 9.95

TO LOVE AGAIN by Evelyn Kennedy. 208 pp. Wildly romantic
love story. ISBN 0-941483-85-1 9.95

IN THE GAME by Nikki Baker. 192 pp. A Virginia Kelly
mystery. First in a series. ISBN 1-56280-004-3 9.95

AVALON by Mary Jane Jones. 256 pp. A Lesbian Arthurian
romance. ISBN 0-941483-96-7 9.95

STRANDED by Camarin Grae. 320 pp. Entertaining, riveting
adventure. ISBN 0-941483-99-1 9.95

THE DAUGHTERS OF ARTEMIS by Lauren Wright Douglas.
240 pp. A Caitlin Reece mystery. 3rd in a series.
ISBN 0-941483-95-9 9.95